For any inquires my contact is-

Email- majansen623@gmail.com
Instagram- King_JansenJansen
Snapchat- King_mattjansen
Facebook - Matthew Jansen

Inspired by true events!

DISCLAIMER

This book does contain mild language and realistic events that people have or are going through. If you know anyone who is dealing with any depression or mental illness, please talk to someone. There is nothing wrong with seeking help to help yourself out. If you or anyone you know is contemplating suicidal thoughts, please call your local emergency number. Just a reminder, The Suicide hotline number is always open 24/7. Their number is 1-800-273-8255. We care about you and we want to make sure you are safe. Thank you and enjoy the book.

Table of Contents

PROLOGUE

Here I am lying down on my bed with the black desk light turned on, and my music on low volume. I look up at the white ceiling with black cracks going every which way. As my eyes try to follow the cracks on the ceiling, I feel something on my cheeks. Tears are rolling down both sides of my face hitting the pillow behind me. This was my final breaking point. Everything I have tried to do has gone to dust. Everyone whom I have met has either left me or hurt me. Every like or comment I have received has only resulted in loneliness.

I try to tell myself that things will get better, but when? I ask myself, Is this how it is going to be? Do I have to keep pretending to be happy for people? Will anyone be there for me when I need them? I keep asking myself these questions, but no answers. I try to think positive about the things around me, but the pain won't let me. As I lay on the bed, I scream, "why me, please," as the tears keep rolling down my cheeks. A few minutes go by, and I decide it's time to go to bed. I get up to turn off the lamp, then lay back down. As I am lying down, I close my eyes and take a deep breath. As I do this, I tell myself, tomorrow will be better, but in my mind, I know that this battle will still be between me, myself, and I.

1
Let's Begin

The sun starts to rise above the small town of Washington, Missouri. The birds are chirping loud in the sky. It's a warm sunny morning. I wake up to the sound of my alarm ringing on my wooden desk. I press the snooze button and roll over back to sleep mode. A few minutes later, I hear my mom calling my name to get up from the kitchen. I yell,

"I'm up mom," with a weak voice. I get out of bed, stepping on my dog's tail, which resulted in me falling on my butt.

"Sorry, spike," I say to him as he looks irritated with me. Spike is a golden lab that we adopted from the rescue pound. He is 2 years old, and I am so happy we got him. After I fall, I get up to head to the bathroom. I look in the mirror with a very groggy face knowing that this is my life. Before I turn on the shower, I put on Taylor Swift because we can all use a little shaking off before we start the day. Once I get out of the shower, and I put on a nice leather jacket with blue jeans and brown boots on. I am feeling very stylish if I do say so myself. I look in the mirror one more time, and I say out loud,

"let's make today a good day." I head downstairs, where I see my mom cooking up an excellent breakfast for me.

"Good morning, sweetie," my mom says in a blissful tone.

"Morning, mom, what are you making?"

"I am making poached eggs with bacon for you."

My mom knows that it is my favorite, but she never cooks it unless there is a special occasion happening. So I ask,

"Is something happening that I don't know about?" She looks at me with a puzzled look then says,

"Today is the first day of my new job, and it is your first day of high school!"

My mom is a nurse at our local hospital but was laid off during the recession in 2008. So in the meantime, she has been taking care of me in all possible ways. You name it she has done it for me. I say to her with much excitement,

"I am so happy for you, and I hope today goes well for you."

I see her smile, and it makes me smile.

"Matt, you are going to be late for the bus, it's 7:30!"

I scarf down my breakfast and run to my mom to give her a hug. I bet you are asking yourself, where is Matt's dad? He died when I was 10 in a car accident during a snowstorm. My dad was going slow on the highway to be safe. The snowstorm was so bad that you couldn't see anything in front of you. This big semi-truck came out of nowhere and slammed him from behind. My dad's car spun around many times before hitting a light pole. My dad died at the scene of the accident. Not a day goes by, where I wish that I could have been there to help my dad. The death was pretty hard on my mother. She didn't come out of the house for a couple of years. Her depression was so bad that she didn't talk to any family members. She has slowly been returning to herself, which has made me happy to see her get back out into the world. As I open the main door with my backpack on, I yell,

"love you, mom," and close the door. As I am waiting for the bus, I am starting to worry a little bit about who I will be meeting. I will not know anyone going to this school since I have transferred schools. My nerves start to get worst once I see the school bus coming up the hill. I see the flashing stop sign turn on, and I ask myself, Is it too late to pretend to be sick?

I go on the bus and sit at the very front near the bus driver, not looking at anyone. I have my headphones in listening to Drake while looking outside the window. Thirty minutes pass, and I arrive at school feeling sick to my stomach. The bus driver opens the door, and of course, with being in the front row, I have to get off first.

I thank the bus driver as I walk down the steps onto the sidewalk of the school. The teachers greet me as I walk into the building. They are formed into a tunnel-like shape leading us to the bleachers. They are clapping and yelling "welcome" and "this will be a great year" and "nice to meet you." I am sitting down, not talking to anyone around me because I am nervous. I see the principal coming to the podium and begin to speak. "Welcome class of 2018, how is everyone?"

This "pep" assembly made me want to go jump off a bridge. The cheerleaders appear on the gym floor to perform a routine that I could've made up in the shower. After seeing that mess of what you call a show, the principal wishes us the best of luck and dismisses us to our classes.

As we were leaving the gym, I put my headphones back in and ignore everyone until I am in my class. I arrive in my history class, and the teacher makes us stand up at the front of the room. Mr. Smith says,

"I want everyone to seat themselves by their last name within 2 minutes."

Everyone is looking at each other, wondering if this man is serious? Soon the room got quiet, and then Mr. Smith yells,

"GO!"

We all start asking the same questions

"What is your last name? "What letter does your last name start with? "Shouldn't I be sitting there, and you are behind me?"

As this is happening, I see Mr. Smith smiling and laughing while we look like chickens with our heads cut off. We hear someone in the background shout,

"thirty seconds left," and there are only three people who are messing this up for us. Within twenty seconds, the three people found their seats, and I am thinking,

"how stupid do you have to be not to know your seat?" I didn't realize that those three people would become my best friends. Nick was sitting in front of me, Henry was behind me, and Calvin was on my right side. We were all laughing as I lean over to Nick and say,

"It's ok; it will only get worse from here." He turns back and whispers,

"yeah, we are all screwed." We both chuckle and then turn our attention to Mr. Smith as he is explaining what we will be learning in class this year. Soon, Mr. Smith gives us the last ten minutes to talk with each other. Nick, Calvin, Henry, and I chat until the dismissal of class. We hit it off so well that I do something that I usually wouldn't do. I am generally not so forward, but I ask, "Do you guys want to sit together at lunch?" They all shake their heads while smiling.

During lunchtime, we all sit together, trying to get to know each other. Calvin is from a military family, Nick's parents are doctors, and Henry's parents are farmers. We are laughing and making great connections. This is the first time where I have genuinely felt like I am a part of a group. Growing up, I was by no means the most popular. I was the odd one out, pretty ugly growing up with the worst case of acne and horrible teeth. No amount of plastic surgery would have helped my confidence that's for sure. I was always so self-conscious that I would hate going out in public. The transition summer from middle school to high school changed me. I received acne medicine that cleared it up within five months. I also had Invisalign that straighten my teeth within a couple of years. I felt good about myself, but still felt like something wasn't there, I just didn't know what.

As lunch comes to an end, I say to everyone,

"we should all hang out sometime." Nick responds with a sarcastic tone,

"Not with a fag like you, haha, just kidding yeah it would be awesome if we did." I laugh and shake off the comment. Henry and Calvin agree to hang out sometime, as well. A few hours later, school comes to an end, and I am back on the bus. I can't believe the day I had. I met these amazing people, and I was so happy. I couldn't stop smiling. I think the bus driver thought I was the joker with how creepy my smile looked in his mirror. Once I get off the bus, I run into the house. I take off my brown boots and slide myself into the kitchen, where my mom is preparing dinner.

"Mom, guess what? I made three new friends today!" Keep in mind, my smile hasn't gone down yet.

"Congratulations, sweetie, how exciting," she says as she puts the pot of pasta noodles on the stove.

As she was cooking, I remember that today was her first day of back to work. I ask,

"So tell me, how was your first day at work?"

She looks up with a big smile as mine and says, "fantastic!." She tells me about all the heart attacks she had to assess, and meeting different types of patients made her day!

"I love doing this job, and I am so happy to be a part of this experience," she tells me. It looks like we both had an eventful day. We sit down in the living room eating the pasta while watching Wheel of Fortune. With how much enjoyment we were having, time flew by fast. It's nine o'clock, and I have to start getting ready for bed. Before I head upstairs, I turn to my mom, and I say,

"I wish today would never end, it was the best day for me." She looks at me with a gentle smile,,

"I'm glad sweetie, there will be plenty more of them to come, now go get some sleep." I kiss her on the cheek and run upstairs. I leap onto my bed with a super comfy soft blanket and pillow set. As I am lying in bed, I thank God for such a beautiful day, but underneath my happiness is a dark world coming.

2
The First Test

Today is the first day of fall, and I can't hold in my excitement. There are three reasons why fall is the best season. One, the leaves on the trees turn into a fantastic art show with all types of colors— red, orange, brown, and yellow. Secondly, I can't wait till I hear the crunch of the crisp leaves underneath my feet as I walk in the streets. Lastly, I am excited about the cold crisp sweater weather. Being able to sit outside with a campfire in front of you while wearing a sweater relaxes me. Thank you mother nature for creating this season. I get up to get ready for school. I look outside my small window to see the leaves starting to change. It makes me so happy to see this. I head downstairs, but I notice a yellow note tab stuck to the table. The note reads,

"Sorry, I am not able to make you breakfast, sweetie today. I was called into work early, Mom". I figured now, with her work schedule being crazy, I guess I should start getting used to this. I take the red apple out of the random place fruit bowl that is in every house ever and head to school.

I arrive at school to see Calvin, Nick, and Henry, all sitting down talking. With a smile, I come up and say

"Hey guys, do you want to go get a snack I'm starving?" Henry looks up from his phone and says,

"I don't have any money." Nick and Calvin are shaking their heads in agreement with him.

"That's ok I can pay for you, it's on me." I didn't think anything about it because I'm just helping out a friend., They look at each other with confused faces, but then Henry said

"Are you sure?" I respond with a smile

"totally." We all receive the breakfast special, which is biscuits and gravy with a side of eggs. When I see them getting the breakfast special, I begin to panic because I didn't know how much money I have with me. I am thinking more about to-go snacks such as a banana or chocolate granola bar. When we all head over to the checkout line, Henry says to the cashier,

"it's ok, it's on Matt," and they all continue to walk away. As I see them walking away, I begin to feel a particular type of emotion.

Maybe nerves? Maybe worried? I'm trying not to think about it too much because this is what friends do, right? The cashier rings everything up and says,

"That will be $17.84" with an unbelievable tone. I give her my student I.D card with my mugshot of a photo on it. She gives it back to me and goes into the kitchen. I head over to the table and sit down. I see that they are halfway done with their meal. I am a little annoyed because they are eating without me. Again, not giving much thought, I am glad I found a good group of friends. The bell rings throughout the building, alerting us that it is time for another day of boring classes. We arrive in our history class, and Mr. Smith announces to the room that it is a movie day. Movie days at our school is never fun because it is always correlated with an essay or some project. Mr. Smith is standing in front of the classroom, starts to talk.

"Ok, guys, we will be watching a movie about World War Two." Everyone in the class moans with disappointment except me. I'm very excited to watch this movie. While we wait for Mr. Smith to put the film up, we begin to make small talk with each other.

I can hear some of my classmate's trash-talking about this movie. One student says to his friend,

"Why do we have to learn this shit?" Another student says,

"I wish I were dead, so I don't have to be here." I look to my right to see Nick muttering something to Henry. Should I be shit-talking this movie as well? Should I pretend to hate this? I whisper for Nick to lean in and tell him,

"This movie will be as good as the crap coming out of my ass," which made Nick laugh pretty hard. As we are laughing, it's as if time froze, and my conscious started to say, "You are so popular, Matt, people like you!" I'm enjoying this moment so much. We hear Mr. Smith say,

"Ok class, the movie is about to begin, please turn yourselves forward." The class grew quiet as the opening scene begins to show. We are watching The Pianist, an authentic masterpiece. Towards the end of the film, you can hear the sniffles and see the tears across the room. Once the T.V. screen went black, the whole place was as quiet as can be. It feels as if someone died, and we are all mourning. Suddenly the room became so bright I felt as if the Sun just blew up in the room without warning. As we try to grasp what has been shown to us, I hear Mr. Smith say,

"Ok class, now I want you to write a 3 page paper on this movie based on what it meant to you." The due date isn't until a few weeks, so I felt like I had plenty of time. When the bell rings for the dismissal of class, we head to lunch. Lunch today is chicken nuggets or corn dogs. This is the holy grail to us at my high school. After I receive my delicious food, I walk up to the check outline. While I am waiting in line to pay, I feel someone touch me. I turn to see who this person is, it is Henry.

"Hey man, what's up?" Henry begins to speak with an underlying tone.

"Matt, I am embarrassed to ask, but could you buy me my lunch?" I reply with a confused tone,

"why?" He looks down and says,

" I don't know if I have enough money for it." I look a little dismayed, but I am not too concerned.

"Yeah, no problem I got you," I tell him. I see him smile, and then we continue to talk while we wait. We arrive at the cashier, and it is the same one who took my breakfast order. Henry tells the lunch lady,

"He is paying for me again" and walks by without a care in the world. As I am waiting to pay, I can sense the lunch lady is not happy with me. She looks at me with a disgusted face and says, "That will be $13.67." I give her $20 with a gentle smile on my face. She takes the money out of my hand very aggressively. Once she gives me my change, I look down and walk away. I arrive at the table and not even a minute passes by when I am asked by Nick,

"Hey Matt, can you buy me candy?" I reply with an aggressive tone,

"I just got here, can I eat?" He says in a joking way,

"No, I want it now." There was a moment of silence, and then he says,

"I'm just messing with you, I will let you eat then you can buy it for me." My nostrils flair as I am releasing a deep breath. I sit down on the cracked blue chair and begin to eat. This is the longest ten minutes of my life because I feel Nick just waiting for me to buy him something. I'm finishing my delicious meal. The moment I stand up to throw away my food, I see Nick getting up as well. I am getting very agitated. I try to remind myself that this is for friendship.

After I throw away my food, Nick and I head over to the candy section. As I am debating between M&M's or Skittles, I see Nick grab M&M's, a Crunch bar and a Laughy Taffy. After a tough decision, I choose M&M's and proceed to the cashier. The cashier says to Nick,

"Love, that is $3.45," and Nick replies,

"That's ok; Matt has it for me."

I see the cashier staring at me, and I give a soft smile back. I am starting to feel a little irritated by this. I'm getting annoyed by people asking me to buy them things all the time. For some reason, though, I keep telling myself that this is how you gain friends. I give her my M&M packet, and she says,

"That will be $4.80." I give her $5.00. She provides me with my change, and I walk away. This time I left feeling a bit degraded.

The last bell rings for the day I didn't want to stay another minute longer. I'm walking through the halls with my headphones in listening to Sam Smith. I'm about to walk outside when I hear the group call my name,

"Matt, Matt, wait," I tried to ignore them by turning my music up. Soon, I hear Calvin's voice saying

"Matt, hold up, please." I take my headphone out of my right ear and say

"I am tired, what's up?"" With a hostile tone. As Calvin is getting his breath back, he says, "Do you want to go to the movies tonight to see Insidious?" I reply with excitement,

"Hell yeah, I love scary movies." I see Nick and Henry in the background, and I ask Calvin,

"Are they going to come?" He looks back at them, and I see them nod. Henry nods his head up and down to that question. I hear my bus number being called, and I head towards the bus. Before I get on the bus, I turn around and yell to Calvin,

"Ok, I will see you guys tonight."

Thirty minutes later, I arrive at my house. I open the door, and I hear the paws of Spike running towards me full speed. I drop my backpack on the ground and plop down. Spike is very excited to see me; he jumps on me and gives me many kisses. After a couple of minutes of playing with Spike, I went into the kitchen, where I look for a can of Pringles. I am relaxing on the couch, watching some news when my phone started to go crazy. *Ding* *Ding* *Ding* *Ding* I pick up my phone to see who is texting me They are all sending me messages about how great of a person I am. I start to lose my tension and become a little bit more grateful to the group. I reply with,

"Thanks, guys, see you later tonight." I didn't think anything of it beside them being kind to me. I put my phone on do not disturb and begin to doze off. I wake up sitting on my bed, but I'm not alone. I see Calvin, Henry, and Nick, all on their phones around my bed. I ask in a faint voice,

" What are you guys doing here?," but they don't respond. For some reason, they could not hear me, yet I could see everything that they were doing. I hear a soft dinging sound and wonder if that is my phone. I look at my phone, but it isn't mine. I am baffled by the whole situation. I get up from my bed and head over to Henrys' phone. I see Henry smiling and laughing so hard. I can't get his attention, so instead, I take his phone out of his hands. I notice that they made a new group chat without me called Using Matt. I read a text saying,

"We are only using Matt for his money." I see Calvin's response with,

"screw that rich fag." I drop Henrys' phone on the ground, and my heart begins to pound hard and fast. I have never felt like this before. I stumble toward my bed, tripping over my own feet. I fall to the ground in pain. I look up and see the group watching over me saying in unison,

"We don't want you. We don't care about you" over and over. I close my eyes as tight as I can, telling myself it's just a nightmare. The tighter I close my eyes, the louder the saying is getting. A couple of seconds pass by, and I hear a woman's voice faintly say,

"Matt, wake up." I keep hearing the woman's voice. I try to locate it, but I can't find it. I finally yell,

"JUST LEAVE ME ALONE!" and suddenly it is as if that was the magic word to end this nightmare. Darkness turns into the light once again. I feel someone touching me while asking me if I am all right. I am sweaty and panting as if I just ran a marathon. I look to my side and see my mom with an anxious look on her face. She says,

"Matt, are you ok?" I tell her,

"I don't know, I had this crazy dream or whatever you want to call it." She wants me to say to her what it was, but I don't want too. I lean over to my phone to see what time it is,

"shit, the movie is in 20" I yell nervously I see on my notifications that the group chat is wondering where I am at. I reply,

"Sorry, guys, took a nap on my way now." I change into sweats because who cares about how you look at the movies, no one can see you. I put my headphones on and put on my playlist. I am riding my new red and blue bike to the movie theatre, which is about 10 minutes away. I arrive at the movie theatre with just 5 minutes to spare. I pull up near the old rusted bike rack to lock up my bike. As I am locking up my bike, I hear,

"Matt, come on, let's go!" I look up to see the group smiling and waving to me. While I am walking towards them, I take a couple of deep breaths and tell myself that I knew I had nothing to worry about, they are my real friends or least I thought so.

3
The Storm

As I am walking up to the group, Calvin says to me,

"How was your nap, jackass?" I reply back with a sarcastic tone,

"I don't know; you should ask your mother." Nick and Henry goes crazy by saying,

"whoah" and "he got you."

It feels pretty good when you can make multiple people laugh. I don't go out of my way to make comments like that, but the group has made me more confident. It is now 7:26 p.m., and we still haven't bought our tickets yet. As we are walking to the door, I pulled out my phone to send a message to my mom. I am letting her know I should be home around 10:00 p.m. As I am texting my mom, I run right into the glass door. I drop my phone and yell,

"shit" out loud. I rub my hand on my head and feel a small bump. The group thought it was hilarious and began to laugh. I say to them,

"Haha, so funny little shits." Then Nick says while screaming, "We aren't the one who ran into the door, dumbass."

I have nothing to say because that is what happened. I wish there could be an app that tells us to look up when we are near a door; that would be nice. We walk inside the movie theatre, and it looks very nice. They had a beautiful bright red carpet to guide us to the ticket area with upcoming movies along the wall. I see Pitch Perfect 2 on there, and I wonder how funny Rebel Wilson is in this one? It is Rebel Wilson, she can breathe, and it's hilarious. I can't wait for the movie to come out. As we are waiting in the line for our tickets, I see the ticket holder signaling us to come forward. I approach the window and see a man wearing a black bow tie with a black vest and white button-down. He says in a very modest tone,

"Hi, how can I help you?" I speak with a gentle tone, "Yes, one ticket for insidious."

"One ticket for Insidious?" he asks. I reply,

"Yeah," but I'm stopped abruptly. I check behind me, and it was Calvin.

"What?" I ask with a confused tone. He leans to me and says,

"This is awkward, but I don't have enough money, could you help me out?" With an unpleasant tone, I yell,

"Are you kidding me? Why don't you ask Henry or Nick?" Calvin looks at them and comes up with a bullshit answer. "

They only have enough money for them." As you can imagine, I am very irritated, but because I was in public, I can't do much.

I release a profound sigh and say,

"fine."

I turn to the young gentleman and tell him,

"Two tickets, please." He presses it on to the register. "Okay, so two tickets to Insidious, that will be $16." I am pissed to the bone. I was planning on spending the $20 on a ticket and snacks. I can't believe I am going to watch a movie without anything to bite on. You can't enjoy the experience of a film without paying a ridiculous amount of money for food and drinks. I see the tickets coming up from the ticket slider, and the worker grabs them. He rips half of the card and gives the other half to me.

"Thank you, and enjoy your movie." I gave him a pissed look and walked away. Henry and Nick receive their tickets, and we head into the theatre. As we walk in, almost every seat is filled. We are wandering up and down the aisle to find a place to sit. We see three seats together in the front row. Henry, Calvin, and Nick run to get the three seats together while I am standing looking very puzzled.

"Sorry, Matt, you should have moved quicker," says Nick. I'm incredibly pissed off at this point, especially at Calvin because I bought his ticket for him. He should have offered his seat to me.

"It's whatever," I tell them with an irritated tone.

I sit down in the chair across the aisle that has soda stickiness on the arm handle. I turn over and see the group having a good time while I'm over here sitting next to grandma and grandpa. Maybe I should have pretended to be their grandson, so they would have bought me popcorn. We are watching the previews for the other upcoming movies. Jesus, how long do they have to be? Why rush to a 7:30 showing when the film won't even start until 8:00. I could have run home and back, and we still would have been watching previews for the newest overrated action movie. The film begins, and of course, I'm in love with Rose Byrne and Lin Shaye. Without these two amazing actresses, we would not have the Insidious we know. Throughout the movie, I jumped and screamed throughout the scary parts. As I'm acting like a little girl in my chair, I turn in my seat to see the group smiling and laughing together. I did not want to admit to myself, but I think it is becoming clear that I am just the punching bag. I try to push that thought out of my mind. After an hour and forty-three minutes later, I could not wait for the next film. The movie ends on a cliff hanger, and I want to know what is going to happen to the family. The lights flicker on, and people begin to leave the theatre. I allow the two people sitting next to me to go first. I cross over the aisle to see the group.

"How did you like the movie?" I ask, and Henry responds by saying,

"It was good." Calvin and Nick both agree by nodding their heads.

As they are getting up from their seats, I see a text on Henry's phone called The Ballers. Henry doesn't know that I am waiting behind him. He slides open his phone, and I swear I see my name with a poop emoji right next to it. Nick coughs as if he is giving a sign to Henry. He looks back and turns off his phone as quick as lightning.

"What, dude, why are you in my space?" says Henry.

I tell him my bad and begin to walk up the aisle. Nick, Henry, and Calvin are whispering to each other about ten feet behind me. We go outside, and I head towards my bike without saying a word.

"Matt, where are you going?" asked Nick. I reply with a fake cough,

"I have to get home. I'm not feeling well." I hear Henry say from a distance,

"Feel better, Matt, have a good weekend."

The other two nod and begin to talk amongst themselves. I unlock my bike from the chain and start to pedal. As I am riding my bike, I am feeling a type of emotion I have never felt before. Overwhelming of sadness? Anger? Both? I can not describe it, but I know it is not happiness. I'm almost home when I hear thunder in the background. I try to pedal faster, but I'm too late. I slam on my breaks to take a breather. As I am panting, a particular smell comes upon me. It is a strong type of scent. Based on the smell, I can tell that the rain is close. I begin to pedal when I see the rain sheer falling down. You can see each streetlight getting darker and darker. The storm is coming towards me at a rapid pace. I'm only ten minutes away from my house. I begin to pedal so fast that I thought I could be apart of the Tour De France. As I am biking down the street, I start to feel big puddles of raindrops hitting me on the back. I am trying my hardest to pedal faster, but I can't. I begin to slow down, allowing the storm to take over me. I am breathing so hard that the side of the stomach is hurting. As the rain comes down harder and harder by the minute, I can't see. I am becoming blind to the objects around me. I try to pedal just a little bit more, but I hit a huge pothole. The pothole makes me lose control of my bike, and I fall off. Instead of getting up, I decide to stay on the ground. If you saw me that night, you would have thought I went swimming with my clothes on. I am soaked, but I didn't care. As I am lying on the ground, an overwhelming sadness kicked in. What is going on? I ask myself. At that moment, I give it to the storm. I burst out crying. I yell,

"Please just leave me alone," but I don't know why I'm shouting that. There is no one else around, just me.

A few minutes pass, and I arrive at the front door. I see that the color of the T.V. screen is still on, which means my mom is still up. This should be fun, I tell myself. I open the door and hear, "Matt, is that you?" My mom comes running to the front door. She says with an angry tone,

"Where the hell were you, and why are you soaked?" I lie to her and say,

"I got lost, okay, my phone died." She looks at me with doubt,

"It's late, get ready for bed." I didn't hesitate at all. While I am heading upstairs, my shoes make a squishing sound every step I take. I took off all my clothes and put them in the laundry basket by my door. I head to the shower, but this time with no music. This is the most depressing shower that I have ever taken. I get out of the shower, dry off, and put on my pj's. I flopped into bed and laid my phone on my desk.

I tell my phone,

"Hey Siri, play Sad Song by Christina Perri. As I hear this song playing, I begin to softly cry so that my mom doesn't listen to me. The tears are as big as an elephant. For some reason, I can't let this pain go. I try to sniffle quietly, but I let it all out. The pain that was coming out of my mouth was loud. Is this normal, crying yourself to sleep? I ask myself. I have never done this before. As the song finishes up, I take a long deep breath in and sigh. I lay on my back, and my eyes are facing the ceiling. The last few tears in me flow down the sides of my cheek. I know this isn't who I am, I'm not myself, but I'm doing it to keep my friends.

4
Happy New Year

A couple months have gone by, and it's finally winter break. I couldn't be any more excited. With all the negativity and feeling sad, I could use a break from people. New Year's Eve is here, and I can't contain my excitement. I believe this holiday is one of the most underrated holidays out there. I hear people say, "What is the point of this holiday? We get closer to death." or "What is the point of celebrating another year going by?" I love New Year's because it gives me hope that the New Year will be better than the last. Some people may not get to live another year. You should be grateful for being around the people who love and cares about you. My mom and I turn on the New Year's Rockin' Eve party with Ryan Seacrest on ABC 30. It has become a tradition for my mom and me to enjoy this time with each other. The time came for the legendary Taylor Swift to perform. She is the last performer before the ball drop. The whole house shakes as I blare the T.V sound. Once she wraps up her performance, Ryan Seacrest comes on and yells,

"time for the countdown!" As the countdown begins, I ask my mom with a worried tone,

"Wait, where is spike?" she says,

"He's upstairs sleeping."

I run upstairs so fast, open the door, and grab him as if there was a fire in the house. I run back down the stairs, and I hear on the T.V – 11,10,9,8. We have our hats on our heads and confetti poppers in our hands. Soon it was 3..2..1... HAPPY NEW YEAR! The house erupts into a chaos of yelling and confetti poppers popping. I can't believe that it is 2016! I'm glad to leave 2015 behind and take on 2016.

It is the first morning of 2016, and I wake up at 10 a.m. I am so tired from staying up so late. As I am walking downstairs, I see the mess that we have created from last night. I clean up for my mom as she is at the grocery store. All the party poppers, food crumbs, and drink spills have been clean up. I give myself a pat on the back for a job well done. I turn on the T.V. to see if there is anything useful for it. As I am flipping through the channels, I stumble across the news channel. The headline reads– Presidential debates dates soon to be released- I can't believe that we are about to vote for a new president. I should mention the area where I live is a conservative town. We are a 'rural' area to the government, so don't be so surprise when Missouri turns red. Since it is winter break, I want to relax and not talk about anything stressful. The holidays should be happy, peaceful, and filled with love, not hate and anger. I have the T.V. music station on while I am sitting in front of the campfire, listening to the wood crackle under the heat. I look outside, and I see white flakes falling from the sky.

"SNOW!" I scream with pure joy! I run upstairs and grab my light blue sweater with black joggers and red snow cabin socks. I make a cup of hot chocolate in a snowman red and white mug. I make sure to top it off with extra whip cream, but I never tell my mom. As I see these large hamster size snowflakes fall from the sky onto the ground, it puts me in such a peaceful state of mind. It is as if my mind forgets about the problems that I am dealing with. I didn't realize how long I was staring at the snow falling because the ground goes from green to white in a couple of minutes.

I hear someone's keys jingling from the outside door; mom must be home. I open the door for her, and I see her hands are full of bags. I lean down to take some of the bags out of her hands.

"Thanks, sweetie," she says with a smile. We walk into the kitchen with the bags and place them on the marble dining set. As we are going through the bags, my mom asks,

"Did you do anything today?" So I reply with

"I just watched the snowfall with holiday music in the background." I'm disappointed that the snowfall ended. She looks pleased and asks,

"Hey, sweetie, after this, would you like to go watch the sunset?" I say with excitement,

"I would love too!" Once we put the bags away, I wait for mom to put on her pj's and make her hot chocolate. We both head onto the patio deck. We sit in our comfortable chairs with a fireplace in front of us. We light the fire and watch the sky change color. My favorite time to view the snowfall is when it hits dusk hours. The sky illuminates a light purple mixed with a beautiful blue. The sun produces a blissful light that creates a breathtaking view. Scientist says it takes 70 to 100 minutes for dusk to complete its full cycle. These are the best 70 to 100 minutes that nature provides.

As we are enjoying the moment my mom asks me,

"Did you know that this was what I used to do with your father?" I shake my head from side to side. She explains to me that when I was little, he would go out to the woods and cut down fresh firewood for us. The smell of oak would linger throughout the house. When my dad was done, he would come inside to grab us.

"Close your eyes, guys," he said as he would guide us outside. Once we were out, my dad would whisper,

"Okay, it's time," and we opened our eyes. We look in awe at the trees wrapped with white lights from the bases to the tips. We heard something making a little crackling noise and look down at the fire pit with a mini Christmas tree on the ground. There were three stockings hooked onto the fire pit with our names on them. We get closer to the fire pit to see three plates full of chocolate chip, sugar, and oatmeal cookies, with three glasses of milk sitting along the stone edge. We would always enjoy the gift of nature together as a family. Now with him gone, I feel like this is how my mom and I can reconnect with him.

I look at my mom with a gentle smile, and I reach over to grab her hand. I tell her,

"Mom, I am always going to be here for you. No matter what, I love you."

She leans over for a hug. We both look up at the small snowflakes falling down. After a few minutes past, we decide that it is time for bed. We fill a bucket of water and pour it on the fire pit. I can hear the sizzling of the fire diminishing. My mom is inside, washing her mug in the sink. I come inside, closing the patio deck door behind me. As I walk past her, I say, "Thanks for a wonderful evening,

Mom, I love you so much." She turns off the sink and looks at me. She says with a peaceful tone,

"You are such an incredible son, never forget that. Now, go to bed," with a chuckle. I head up the stairs and jump onto my bed. Spike comes running in behind me and climbs on top of me. After a couple of minutes of rubbing his tummy, I decide it's time to go to bed. I put my body under the covers while I have spike lying on the right side of me. I pet him a couple of times to calm myself down. As I'm in bed, I am telling myself what a great break this has been. I haven't had to deal with any hate, anger, or drama. This was the most peaceful feeling I have ever felt. It's a shame that this feeling won't last forever, but maybe one day.

5
Welcome back

Today is the first day of school since winter break. It is torture getting out of bed. I am so slow and dead inside. I just want to stay in bed and pretend that I am sick. A few minutes go by, and I decide that it is officially time for me to get up. I get up from my bed and stretch my legs out. As I am stretching, a loud yawn comes out of my mouth. What happened to me over winter break? I ask myself. I skip showering and just put on some sample cologne that I received from a perfume shop. I walk into the kitchen to take a banana from the fruit bowl. I think Rachel Ray or Martha Stewart told every woman that they need this piece of crap on the table. As I am walking to the bus stop, I put my headphones in and begin to listen to Lorde's album Pure Heroine. Her voice is so mesmerizing with how subtle it is. While I am waiting at the bus stop, I can't help notice that I am full-on dancing in the street. I don't even care that my neighbor looks at me with a confused face; I dance even crazier. I see the bus pulling up the hill, and that is when I collect myself. As I enter the bus, I say, "good morning" to the driver and sit down. For some odd reason, I can not stop dancing in my seat to the music. Thanks, Lorde.

I arrive at the beautiful hell hole, I mean school. The bus driver opens the door, and I hop off the bus. As I am walking into the building, I look around to see if there is an open table. My eyes keep scanning up and down until I see them sitting down. I recognize the group who I 'haven't spoken to since last year sitting at the back table. Since this is the only table that isn't full, I head over to them. As I am walking over to them, I am holding a slight grin upon my face. I put my trey down on the grey circle table, and I say

"is it cool if I sit here?" They all look at each other then back at me, and Calvin says,

"I guess." I can feel some tension since I left them for a while. I don't know why they are mad at me when they left me crying my ass off on the side of the road. I did nothing to them to treat me like this, but I guess some people don't grow up. I inhale a deep breath and say,

"guys 'I'm sorry." They looked up at me and allowed me to continue what I have to say.

"I'm sorry for leaving not telling you about how I was feeling I just don't like to share my emotions with people." Henry begins to speak,

"Why 'didn't you tell us you wanted a break?" I look down at my food then back up. I tell them with a discouraged tone,

"I don't know I guess I was embarrassed, I was never a part of a friend group before, so I don't know how to communicate well when issues come about." I want to tell him that I 'don't have to tell you guys everything that I am doing or feeling, but that would have made the situation worse. There is a moment of silence with everyone feeling a little unease. I break the ice and say,

"Are we just going to act like children, or are we going to talk?" With an aggressive tone, Henry takes a deep breath and stares at me with content. He expresses that the group cares about me and how I am not alone. Calvin interrupts Henry and says,

"The whole point of friendships is so that we can build each other up and create memories that will last for a lifetime." I never thought of it that way because I never had a safety net of restoring to someone if I have an issue. As Calvin wraps up with his ted talk, I continue to nod and act as if I am listening. We hear the first bell ring, which means it's time to clean your tables. Nick says,

"Wait, did you guys see these new apps called Instagram and Snapchat?" Henry replies with a confused tone,

"No, what are they?" Kevin says

"So Instagram is a social media app that you share your photos online to people, and people can follow you and like them while Snapchat is a texting app where you take photos and send to your friends."

We have a silent couple of seconds, and then we all grab our phones out. We head over to the app store and begin to search for Snapchat and Instagram. I download them both within a few seconds. I am smiling from ear to ear because I am thinking that this is my chance to finally make new friends and see what my other classmates are reposting.

The bell rings for a second time, which means we have to go to the classroom now. The whole table gets up to throw away their food scraps then head to class. I tried to be like Kobe and shot my milk carton from 30 feet away. I yell,

"K.O.B.E.," and I see the friend group eyes look at me. I throw it but miss it by a long shot. Kevin turned around and says,

"Kobe my ass," with a sarcastic tone. We both laugh and head towards the class. When we enter the classroom, we notice that Mr. Smith isn't here. I ask another student in the room

"Yo, do you know where Mr. Smith is?" She replies with a slight hesitation,

"I think he is at the hospital with his wife as she gives birth." I have a surprised expression on my face. We see this older woman walk in. She is wearing a blue and white zig zag skirt with a black belt along her waist with a white button-down. As she is placing her purse down, she says,

"Good Morning class" with a peaceful tone.

"Good morning," we all reply in sync with a dreadful tone. She has her back towards the whiteboard and begins to write something on the board. My name is Mrs. Gomez, as she points to the board.

"I will be your substitute teacher for today as Mr. Smith is out" with an eager tone. A moment goes by then she says

"Okay I see here on the worksheet that today is a free day for you guys, so please work on school work and do not play any games, if you need me I will be up here" Henry, Calvin, Nick, and I all turn our desk towards each other and already had one thought in mind— Social media. We open our phones, and we first go to Instagram. After we are doing signing up, we get to the page that shows us who to follow.

"I'm going to follow the Falcons," says Nick.

"I'm going to follow Lebron," says Calvin.

"I'm going to follow the Nature channel," says Henry. We all look at him with a confused look, but he says,

"I'm just messing with you, Post Malone, following." They look at me and ask

"Who is going to be your first following" with a sarcastic tone. I look down, and I see The Chain smokers. I say

"I love the Chainsmokers, bam, following" as I show Henry my phone. I'm happy to feel like I am a part of something. Soon I start to see some of my classmates here with weird user names such as "Dilf_69" or "Unicorn slave" or "Nah bisshhh_blessed. As I am reading these user's names, I feel like I am getting cancer with how bad these user names are. A moment passes where I start to see the dark blue heading that says, "follow" turns into a white "follow." I start to see the 'popular' students on my list, and I see this as an opportunity. I click follow on each of their names while I do this, I begin to feel butterflies in my stomach. What if they don't follow me back? What if they think I am a stalker? A few seconds go by, and I feel my phone vibrate. I look down, and I see those whom I followed are beginning to follow me back. It gives me a warm feeling knowing that I am making all these 'friends.' The teacher gets up from her desk and begins to walk around the classroom. The group put their phones away and pretends to discuss the essays we had to write over The Pianist.

"How is everything going over here," Mrs. Gomez says with a smile. We all make eye contact, and I tell her, "We are great, just trying to compare whose paper is better. "My paper is the best out of them all," said with an attitude. I hear a couple of pff's and laughs from the group. While Mrs. Gomez chuckles and says, "Well, it looks like you guys are working hard, keep it up," then she leaves.

We are laughing very hard since we pulled that out of our asses. We grabbed our phones out again and decided to head onto Snapchat. We try to create unique snapchat names such as "cakes1todough1" or "Wet_frankie99", mine was "Mjrox123. At that time, I thought spelling rocks with an X would make me look cooler to the popular kids. Just like Instagram, Snapchat provided me with recommendations from my contacts. I start to see the group's user names pop up and of course, the popular ones again. I start to click add friends, and the handle would say, "added." That warm feeling of being accepted was kicking in again. The school day is coming to an end, and everyone is parting their ways. Nick says

"I'll make a group chat on Snapchat later on tonight" we all respond with "dope," and we all went home.

As I am on the bus, I am starting to get freak out over who has followed me and who hasn't. Why should I care about this? I don't talk to most of them anyway, what's the difference. This is social media; that's the difference. It has a different way of making us feel better about ourselves. It makes us more confident to post a more flattering post that we usually wouldn't. It gives us a "safe" space knowing that this is my profile, and I'm the only one who has control of it. It makes us feel as if we have a particular type of responsibility or bar to set. Social media has allowed us to share the fake side of yourself instead of who we really are.

I arrive home to see a package on the doorstep. The box is to my mom, I think it is her new coffee maker. I open the door and head into the kitchen, where I place the package on the table. I walk over to the fridge to grab a Dr.Pepper. While I am in the middle of reaching the can, I hear multiple dings at a rapid pace. I run over to my phone to see that I have over 20 notifications from Snapchat and 50 from Instagram. I yell with such excitement. Spike hears me and comes running down the stairs and barks out of control. I say,

"yes, Spike, that's right. I'm finally likeable" with such joyfulness. Wow, what is happening to me? Just a few months ago, I wasn't caring about who approves of me, but now I want to know. I open Instagram first to see who followed me back. As I am scrolling through, I suddenly stop in my tracks. I see six popular students who start to follow me. I can't tell you how happy I am! I start to freak out and start asking myself, "wait, is this real?" and "They don't talk to me in person why now?" Screw it, I thought, people actually care about me. I head over to Snapchat, and I see the 20 people' friended' me. I realize that Henry, Calvin, and Nick added with me a couple of random classmates. I keep scrolling down, and I see the same six popular kids added me. I throw my phone down with excitement. I ask myself if I should message them first. I mean I don't want them to think that I care, but I kind of do.

What if I send a sup photo with half my face to show them that I can be chill as fuck. After I take the picture, I send it to my new friends. I see it deliver, and my heart drops. I start to have doubts about me sending the message. What if they don't respond? What if they unfollow me? I try not to get panic, but it is hard for me not too. As I am waiting to see if they opened the message, I check the delivery time. Fifteen seconds went by, thirty-five seconds went by, and now it's a minute. I am starting to get a little doubtful as every second passes by.

"I knew it was too good to be true," I say with an underlying tone. I check once more before giving up, and I stop in my tracks. I see four letters– O.P.E.N.– my inner child is going crazy and was starting to freak out just a little bit. I look at the time on the open, and it said 3 minutes ago. I have seconds thoughts about the photo I sent them. What if I have sent them a photo with my shirt off? O, what if I sent them a mirror picture holding my cats' ass up to my face. I think that is a popular thing to do? Maybe? No, don't be silly, Matt, get yourself together. My phone goes black for about eight seconds before I see the logo pop up on my phone, and I hear the ding. My reaction skills were as quick as Usain Bolt at the 2012 Olympics. I open the app, and I see that it was from one of the popular students named Kyle. Kyle is the best baseball player at our school. He is of average height, blonde hair with brown eyes. He is super athletic, so of course, everyone wants to be his friend. Kyle sends me a photo of a full-body being at the gym with a tilted camera with the caption *"Welcome to snap bruh, how's it going?"* I am freaking out since this is the first time all year that we have talked. I know I wasn't up to his level, but maybe I am? Thank you, social media, for making my world a better place. I decide to play it cool, and I send a message of me chilling on the couch with the caption. It's okay, I am about to make dinner. Within a minute of the text being sent, he opens it and responds with a smiley face. I hear the door opening, and I try to recollect myself.

"Hi, mom," I say with such excitement. I know she feels it because then she says,

"Hi, I assume school went well today?" I try to stay claim, but it didn't work. I spoke with a loud voice,

"I am becoming popular at school with many people following me on social media." She replies with a surprising look,

"Wow, look at my baby go, keep it up, sweetie." For dinner tonight, I will let Mr. Popular choose what we should eat. Instead of us making something tonight, my mom and I went to TacoBell across the street. After our fabulous meal, we head back home to get ready for bed. Before I head upstairs, I tell my mom I love her and give her a kiss on the cheek. I am in my room, where I plug in my phone and hop into bed. I turn on some chill music and begin to relax. As I am starting to fade into a sleep slumber, I begin to feel a little anxious. Should I snap everyone a goodnight post before I head to bed, I ask myself. I grab my phone off the desk and take a photo of me with half my face on a pillow. I caption it, What a day, blessed to be in bed, have a good night. I send it to my 20 followers on social media. After it reads deliver, turn off my phone and put it back on my desk. I rolled back over on my pillow, and I feel the day letting go. I start to toss back and forth more than ever. I think my heartbeat is pacing quicker. Was I nervous about who will respond? Was I worried about how many people would react? I guess we will find out in the morning.

6
The Approval

It is five o'clock in the morning, and I wake up more anxious than ever before. I grab my phone off the desk as quick as I can. I don't think you understand the importance of this situation. This is a matter of life or death. I turn over my phone to see that I have 11 notifications from Snap chat. I exhale with relief I scroll through to see who did respond and who didn't. I click on the names of those who responded to me. They are lying in bed with a caption "You as well man see you later." Others responded with a photo of the T.V on with the caption "thanks." I continue to scroll to see that I am a part of a group called Asswipes. I am trying to figure out why they chose this name. This must be the group chat Calvin made. I am so blessed to have such great friends who want me to be a part of their group.

As the bus is pulling into the school, I couldn't contain my smile. After receiving the number of responses, I feel like people are beginning to care about me. Instead of walking into the cafeteria this morning, I decided to take a walk. I head over to the park next to the school. The sun is mixing with the light grey clouds to put on a beautiful show. I see an old wooden bench next to a big oak tree in the middle of the park. I sit down on the bench before class starts. While I am sitting, I have an artistic idea that pops into my head. I get up from the bench to get closer to the oak tree. I grab my phone out of my backpack and put it on the ground. Since I don't have anyone to take my photo, I have to get creative. I take off my right shoe and place it on the ground in front of me. Then I put my phone inside my shoe, aiming the camera right at me. I know what you are thinking, and yes, my cameraman is better than yours. I am trying different poses before I hit the countdown button. I try looking relaxed up against the tree, I put my arm over my head, and I put one leg up while sitting straight up. I click the countdown button on my phone and go into position. 3..2..1.. flash, my 'photoshoot' is over with I check my camera roll to see the masterpiece. As I am checking my photos, I hear the bell ring. I turn off my phone and head to class.

I arrive in class with one minute to spare. I see my classmates looking right at me.

"Matt, where were you? says Henry.

"I was sitting in the park before class." I don't know why they care about where I was.

"Have you finished your paper on World War Two."

"O crap, I didn't finish it," I say with panic in my voice. I see Mr. Smith walking into the classroom. I try to think of excuses before he comes to collect our papers. Should I tell him that my dog ate my computer or that my grandma deleted my files? Mr. Smith puts his bag down and says

"Good Morning, class. I hope you have your papers out ready for me to collect them." Everyone, but for me, has their papers on their desks. Mr. Smith begins to walk around to collect the reports.

"Thank you, Alice, Thank you, Toby, Thank you Nick" Mr. Smith arrives to me,

"Um, Matt, where are your papers?" I try to think of an excuse right on the spot.

"I don't think I was here when you assigned this homework." Nick interrupts me,

"No, you were here remember we were discussing it." I turn my head straight at Nick and say,

"Thank you, man, shouldn't you be working on next week's homework? Mr. Smith looks at me with disappointment in his eyes,

"Matt, did you forget to do the assignment?" I guess I should tell him the truth. I put my head down and say,

"Yes, I thought it was due later, my apologies." Mr. Smith is contemplating on what he should do to me.

"Listen, the actual due date is tomorrow at 8am, can you bring it in then?" I shake my head rapidly up and down. While Mr. Smith walks away, I see Nick shaking his head with jealousy. I just smile and look to the front of the class.

The school day comes to an end, and I am back at home. I am chilling on the couch while scrolling through my phone. I head over to the photos I took earlier today. I am debating on which photo I would like to put up on my social media. I pick the picture with my knee up while my arm is resting on it. Since I can't decide, I go to the group chat to get their approval. I begin to write my message,

"Hey guys, I need your approval about this photo what do you think?" Nobody responses for a couple of minutes. I see that Calvin is online. Calvin begins to type,

"Matt, are you a model, hot stuff, haha." Then I see Nick and Henry are both online. Nick begins to type,

"Bruh, this is so generic, but not bad." Henry dittos it and says,

"I peed on that tree once; otherwise, I like the photo." I write back,

"I don't care if I sat in your pee, I have to do it for the gram." Nick response with a rolled eyes emoji.

I head over to my social media profile to upload the photo. As I am editing my photo to its' perfection, I can't help but think about something. Why did I have to seek approval for my photo? Shouldn't I have uploaded without the judgment of others? I upload the photo, and I feel happy about it. Not only because it is a great photo, but because I know that I will have people approving it. I feel like I need to have the approval of others to be liked. For me to succeed on social media, I have to receive the approval of others. I love this happy, warm feeling, but I know that this isn't what true happiness feels like.

7
First Like

Before my shower, I put on Taylor Swifts Red album. You can say what you want about her, but she is a goddess in my eyes. After the shower, I check my phone to see what the temperature is outside. It is currently 26 degrees with sunny skies. So I don't freeze to death, I chose to wear these black boots with blue jeans and a red sweater. After feeling very stylish, I head downstairs to another note on the kitchen table. The message writes out,

"Good morning, Mr. Popular, have to go to work early; love you." I let out a little chuckle and threw the note into the trash. I have plenty of time to make a proper breakfast before school starts. I grab the skillet from below the stove. I turn on the oven to a medium temperature and place the skillet on top of the heater. I open the refrigerator and grab the giant carton of eggs. I crack open three eggs.

"Damn it," I yell as pieces of the eggshell fell into the bowl. I begin to try to pick up the pieces, but they keep slipping out of my fingertips. After a couple of tries, I give up and start mixing with them inside the bowl. A little crunchy omelet won't hurt me. While I am combining the bowl, I yell out loud,

"Hey Siri, play pop music." There is a moment of silence then I hear,

"Ok, now playing pop music," Siri says with a calm voice. Within a split second, I detect the tune to Cardi B's hit single Bodak Yellow come on. I start going crazy, hearing this queen rap her butt off. I throw the whisk up into the air allowing it to fall on the ground. I begin to dance hardcore like never before. As I get towards the end of the song, I start smelling some type of a burning smell. I yell so loud,

"shit the eggs." I look down to see my eggs burned to the core. I grab the skillet and head over to the trash can leaning against the wall. The smell of brunt eggs is never pleasant. I grab an apple off the table and head to the door. Before I head out, I grab my tan trench coat and kiss Spike on the nose.

"Jesus is it cold as hell outside," I say out loud. I put on my headphones and begin walking to the bus stop. I see the bus coming up the hill while I am waiting at the stop sign. I step onto the bus and place my butt down on the seat.

I arrive at school to see the Asswipes sitting their usual spot.

"Morning asswipes," I say with a smile. Henry looks at me and says,

" I see you saw the group name" with a condescending tone. I ask,

"Why did you guys pick that name?" Nick replies with a tone, "why did your parents name you the way they did little bitch, boy?" I look at him and laugh while saying,

"Alrighty, then." We are all on our phones, and Calvin says out of nowhere,

"Bruh, should I post this on insta?" It is a picture of him eating a sandwich with his dog taking a crap in the background. I look at him and say,

"dude, your dog, hmm." He turns the phone towards himself and says,

" That damn little bastard." We are laughing so hard that the people around us are telling us to shut up. Once we collect our breaths, Henry motion us to lean in as he shows us what his profile consists of. His profile contains pictures of his dogs, family, himself, and vacation spots he has been too. The number of likes he is getting on each of his images is ridiculous. I grab his phone out of his hand and ask, "How are you getting so many likes on your photos?" He explains to me that the more followers you have on Instagram more like you will be receiving. I open my Instagram to see that I still only have 50 followers. I look at Henry's Instagram, and it says he has over 358 people following him. At that moment, my mindset changed. It is my mission to get more followers than all of these asswipes. Let the best man win.

After a tiring day of school, I finally arrive home. I open the door to see Spike running towards me like he always does. I head into the living room and plop myself down on the couch. After a few minutes of silence, my phone *dings*, it's from the asswipes. I check to see what they are talking about, and it is Nick asking if he should post the photo of his dog's snout in his mouth with his cheeks puffed out. I am about to type to the group chat, but Calvin beats me to it.

"Are you giving your dog a kiss or eating his soul out?" I respond with a laugh out loud emoji.

We see Nick reads it and types, "Can't be both, don't hate." As Nick is about to upload another Instagram photo for the one-hundredth time, I decide that maybe I should upload another one. I look through my camera roll to see pictures of Spike, my family, and myself. I see a picture of half my body showing, like a yearbook photo. I am wearing a white plain shirt with puffed-up hair leaning to the left. My face in the picture looks dazed as if I am thinking about something. I felt that this would be a great photo to share. I open the app to see that my picture is on the screen I see two things on the bottom of the screen- Filter and Edit. I am playing around with the filters to see how my photo can look more spontaneous to my 50 followers, not bragging.

I see a filter for black and white, or Instagram calls it "moon." I click on the 'moon' filter, and I thought it's a great fit, simple and basic. I press next, and now I am supposed to come up with a caption. I sit for a while to think about it. What if I captioned it as "Welcome to my world." I give it a moment of thought and delete it. As I am trying to figure out my caption, inspiration hits me. I decided to title my photo *camouflage* with the thinking emoji. Now I am supposed to use hashtags on Instagram to capture what is in the photo to gain more followers. As I am looking at my picture, and I use the hashtag *#me, #blackandwhite, #eyes, # lips, # hairstyle, and the last one was #sitting*. I feel like the more hashtags I use, the more I am prolonging the photo I am feeling terrific about this photo. As I hit the share button, I feel a little discomfort. I am worried about not receiving a like or a comment. A couple of minutes go by and no notifications yet. Ten minutes go by and still nothing.

"If I were one of the Kardashians, I would have been at one million likes by now," I express with a pissed off tone. Fifteen minutes go by, and now I am regretting this post. I decide to keep my mind off of this I go for a run. I put on my Nike running gear on with a black windbreaker and Nike running tights for men. I grab my red iPod touch and put it on my running playlist. It had all sorts of famous artists– Taylor Swift, Post Malone, Cardi B, The Chainsmokers, Halsey, and many more. I love running to the beat of the songs because sometimes I feel like I am with the artist. It also makes running go by so much quicker, give it a try. About forty-five minutes later, I arrive back at the house, and I see my phone on the counter still. I remove my headphones as I am breathing heavily.

I grab a blue Gatorade from the back of the refrigerator. After I close the door, I am facing my phone. After a few seconds go by, I reach for my phone with my right hand. I flip it over, and the notification screen comes on. I see that I have seven Instagram notifications waiting for me. I swipe to open to the app. At the bottom of my screen, I see three hearts, and four-person figures pop up orange.

I click on my photo, and I see the three people who liked it. I check my follower's list, and it says 53 now. I click on that to see who added me, and it was more kids from school. I begin to feel this warm, loving feeling again. I screenshot this to the group chat and send it to them. I see that everyone sees the photo and starts to type. "I *like that Matt*," wrote Nick, "*Nice one dude*," replies Calvin, and lastly. I see Henry typing. I give him a couple of seconds, and I notice a thumbs-up emoji on my screen. I reply with a bunch of hearts and write back,

" *I am so glad you guys like it.*" I never thought in a million years that I would start caring about how many likes

I get, how many followers I have, or how many comments I receive. Welcome to the dangerous world of social media.

8
First Comment

My eyes are disturbed by the faint of sunlight coming through the window. I forgot that we are getting closer to summer, which means the sun is rising at 6:30 in the morning. I bring my head up to look at the time on my phone. It is for six forty-five in the morning. Lately, I have been waking up way earlier than my alarm. My sleep schedule is not approving of this. I know there is something important today. I grab my phone off the desk and check the date. Today is the debate day at Flint, Michigan, on CNN. I get out of bed and put on my black Birkenstocks. I go downstairs to the living room to turn on the news channel. As the news station is on for background noise, I grab my phone and begin to check out my social media. I notice that my Instagram follower list went from 53 to 70, which I question. I went to see who followed me, and they were followers of Nick, Henry, and Calvin. I am flattered that they want to follow me. I start to look at the recommendation follower list that Instagram gave me. I see that you have Serena Williams, Zendaya, Lebron James I start clicking follow for all of them. I continue down the list, and I stumble on Hilary R. Clinton, Donald Trump, Bernie Sanders, and other politicians. I start clicking on each of their profiles and begin to stalk them. I like their photos in mass numbers hoping that maybe my name will catch their eye on their notifications. I didn't realize how long I have been on social media because I hear my mom say from her bedroom,

"sweetie, it is seven-fifteen. You need to start getting ready for school." I jump from the couch, running up the stairs by twos. I check the weather on my phone as I usually do every morning, and it says the high will be 63 today. I put on a button-down plaid shirt with tan shorts and my Nike shoes on. I head back downstairs and head out the door by seven twenty-two.

As I am on my way to the bus stop, I notice that I am not paying attention to the road because I am on my phone. I start to lean to the right, and I hear a loud honk, it is my neighbor. She rolls down her window and slows down. "Matt, please get off your phone while you are walking; it is dangerous," she says.

"Sorry, Mrs. Taler, hey, are you ready for debate night?" She scoffs,

"Please, it is going to be another clown show." I nod with a smile, but deep down, I had the urge to say,

"Your make up looks like a clown did it." I reply, "alrighty, have a good day at work," and she says, "thanks matt, bye." I arrive at school, and I feel a little uneasy. I think the reason is that I am at a majority conservative school, and with me being a liberal, it doesn't help the situation out. I don't care about what party you stand associate yourself with. Everyone is entitled to their own beliefs as you should be. However, my motto is that I will not tolerate any form of hate towards another person base on their race, religion, background status, or sexual preference. If it is not harming you in any shape, way, or form, leave them alone. It requires so much courage for them to step outside, knowing that they are already a walking target to the public eye. For the love of God, please don't hate someone just because they are different.

While I walk over to the table, I see people whispering and staring at me. I hear my classmates say things like,

"The snowflake here" or "I bet he is going to cry when Hilary loses the election just like all the other liberal babies out there." I am getting a little angry at them, but I try to block the noise out. I haven't been at the table for more than a couple of seconds when Nick turns to me and says, "I think Hillary will be the DNC nominee. I act so surprised and say,

"you are probably right." We start to discuss in a debate who would win Trump or Clinton. As I am talking to Henry, I tell him that Hillary would beat Trump in a debate. He looks at me with such rage and says,

"Are you freaking crazy, Trump would kill her just like Hillary killed the military members in Benghazi."

I try to be polite as I can be, but the gloves are off.

"Fuck off, you know that Trump would be the worst thing for America." He begins to laugh, and says,

"I'll see you later." I get up from the table and head to the bathroom. As I am in the bathroom, I am splashing water on my face. I am trying to tell myself to relax before I say something I will regret. I don't want to lose these friends again, but I don't want to be the butt of all the rude and negative comments. After getting myself together, I leave the bathroom and head to class.

After a long day of fighting off political views from people whom I didn't know, I am finally home. It is annoying to be told your opinions are wrong, and my opinions are right. I am not ready for when it comes time for the actual election. We are a couple hours away from seeing the hopeful Madam President appear on stage. My mom comes into the kitchen and says,

"Matt, I have a surprise for you." I look at her with a confused look at I say,

"Yes?" I notice that she is holding something behind her back. She moves her hands from her back to the front, and it is a box. She says with a gentle smile,

"I think you are going to like what is inside it." I grab the box out of her hands and begin to open it. As I am opening the package, I see the backing of a blue shirt. I grab the object out of the box and flip it towards my face. I can't believe my mom bought me a shirt that says Hillary Clinton 2016, I'm With Her. I drop the shirt on the table and give my mom a big hug. She asks,

"do you like it?" I shake my head a thousand times, yes. She goes back to the kitchen to make some pizza. As I am watching the pre-coverage of the debate, the commentators are annoying me. They think sound appealing to the viewers, but they keep repeating what each other has already said. While the commentators are speaking, I check out social media to see what is happening. I notice at the bottom of my Instagram; I see an orange figure of a heart and person pop up again. The heart reads 24 likes, and the person shows 36 followers. I tap my profile as an overall view, and I see I'm at a total of eighty-six followers. The majority of new followers are the conservatives of my school, with a few liberals. I don't care who follows me as long as I am becoming popular.

I change the channel to CNN as the debate begins. As the commentators are speaking about the rules of the debate, I put on my brand new Hillary Clinton shirt to show my support. While I change clothes, my mom has finished cooking the pizza. I walk out of the bathroom to the smell of melted cheese and pepperoni. I grab a couple of slices head over to the couch. Before I sit down, my mom says,

"Sweetie, hand me your phone? I want to take a photo of you in that shirt." While she is trying to work the camera app, I get up to the tv waiting for the right moment. The commentator tells the audience,

"Please welcome me introduce the DNC front runner and former secretary of state Mrs. Hillary Rodem Clinton."

I tell my mom to get ready as the camera is panning to Hillary.

With a loud voice, I yell,

"Now!" My mom snaps the photo, and I run so fast that I hit my foot against the table legs. I grab the phone out of her hands, and I am in love with how the photo turns out. I tell her that I am going to put this on my social media. I can tell my mom wants to tell me something, but she just keeps smiling. I go to Instagram, edit my photo with the caption "Madam President Hillary Clinton <3 <3 <3" with hashtags #nextpresident, #femalestrong, #Nevergiveup, #Imwithher. After I post the photo, I put my phone on do not disturb. A later, it is pretty clear that Hillary will win the nominee, no doubt. I check back to my phone to see that I have nine Instagram notifications. I swipe right on the unlock screen to open the app. I see four likes, four new followers, but this is new. I see it looks like three lines within a box, I guess that is the comment section. I head straight to my profile to see what they had to say. My internet is being slower than usual. My photo pops up, and I scroll to the bottom where I see a comment from Merica_baby13. I don't know who this person is. I click on the comment section, and what I read leaves me frozen to my core.

"Get this faggot snowflake out here; we need a man to do the job." with a middle finger emoji and angry face. Yup that is my first comment that I will always remember. I hold my phone and let the auto-sleep mode take over within thirty seconds. The only thing I see is my reflection staring at the phone. As my mom is sitting next to me, she notices my facial expression goes from happy to serious within a matter of seconds. She looks at me with concern and asks, "Is everything ok?'

I am trying to figure out why this stranger would say something so rude. I try to brush off the comment and say,

"uh, yeah, uh, I am going to head to bed" with a defeated tone. I give my mom a hug and head upstairs. As I am lying on my bed, I can't stop checking on that comment. I keep reading it over and over again. I thought social media is a place for people to post funny pictures of their animals, family photos, or congratulate people on their success, not spread hate. I am wondering if other people have received comments like this. So I head over to the explore page on Instagram to see a list of celebrities. After seeing Taylor Swift's name pop up, I click on her profile. Beware that this is when she is having her feud with Kanye and Kim for the song the Famous. One person wrote,

"This bitch thinks she is all that when she is a snake." Another person wrote,

"What a disgusting lying pig, good job snake" with a couple of hand clap emojis. I am getting very agitated by every comment I read. Why are we mean to celebrities when they have given us so much? I don't understand why we have to be so hateful towards each other online. I go back to the explore page to see Maria Sharapova's profile. She is one of the best tennis players I have ever seen play. She is releasing a statement to the public after being caught by the WADA's for taking an 'illegal' drug. As the video is finishing up, I look at the comment section to see people ripping her apart. This woman writes,

" This bitch is a cheater, bye-bye Maria." This man, who I am sure is living in his parent's basement wrote,

" It looks like she is Maria Sorrypova today." The last comment I read says,

"She is a disgrace to the tennis community and should not return." I take a moment to realize what I have just read. I feel sorry for celebrities. They have been entertaining us with music, sports, and shows and repay them with hate and negativity. I'm trying to figure out what kind of world we are living in. I put my phone on my desk and begin to fall asleep. For some reason, I am having a hard time falling asleep. I am feeling so tense and angry at the same time. It is not a good idea to read comments before bedtime. I keep rolling back and forth, trying to get into the right position, but nothing is working. Tonight is going to be another long night for me.

9
Word of Wars

It's 3 am, and I can't sleep for the life of me. I'm still pissed about the comment I received. *"Get this faggot snowflake out here, we need a man to do the job,"* keeps replaying in my mind. I grabbed my phone off my desk and went to my profile. I know I shouldn't argue with a stranger, but I will not let him get away with what he said. I begin to think about what I should write back. My thumbs start to type,

"Hey, @Merica_baby13, why don't you stop being a baby and say it to my face?" I think that is a good response, but then I realize that I don't want him to know where I live. So I hit the backspace and begin to think of a better comeback. After a couple of minutes of going back and forth in my head, I finally have the perfect response. I begin to type,

"How about stop eating your twinkies in your mom's basement and actually do something with your life@Merica_Baby13." I feel a little anxious after sending the message. What if he tries to snatch my dog for ransom? What if he gets the Russians to spy on me? Thanks to social media for making me paranoid. After a couple minutes have passed, I see that I have received a new notification from @Merica_baby13. I can't tell you how much rage I am feeling at this point. He claps back by writing,

"@king_jansenjansen You know what you and Indian food have in common? You both give me the raving shits. So why don't you run to mommy and suck on deez nuts." This bastard wants to dance, let's dance bitch boy. Without thinking I message back,

"Hey @Merica_baby13, I hope you know that your beliefs are disgusting. Plus, I don't know what Indian food you're eating, but I know that I am delicious, just ask your mother."

After hitting the send button, I am raging with flames right now. Within a few seconds, I get another reply from @Merica_baby13. He replies with,

"Ok, listen here, jackass, you are the little bitch who has the disgusting views. I do not like you and will never like you. You are an annoying baby millennial who can't afford crap. How about you go and get a job rather than complaining about how bad life is." My jaw drops as my eyes are squinting, trying to figure out who the hell he thinks he is talking too. I begin to smack the keyboards so loud that you can hear it throughout the house. I reply with one middle finger emoji and added,

"No, you listen to me, @Merica_Baby13, how about you stop being an annoying piece of shit. I don't know who you are, but I can tell I could never be around a person like you. How about you get off your ass and do something with your life rather than arguing with a teenager, you wasted cumshot." I will not let anyone insult me or my views. I know I'm in the right, and he is wrong, correct? After I send my response, I decide to block this dude once and for all. I hate the new stress that I am feeling. As I am about to turn off my phone, I feel it vibrating. It is Henry calling me. I answer it, and without a hello, I hear,

"Matt, why are you cursing at someone who you don't even know?" I reply with an angry tone,

"He insulted my views and was taking aim at me." I knew that was a weak excuse, but it's the truth.

"Matt, that doesn't matter. Is he hurting you? Is he making threats to you? No, so why engage with someone like him?" I can tell that Henry is distraught with me.

"I don't know, I guess I felt he was attacking who I am as a person," I tell him with a shaky voice.

"You do realize that I and probably other people have seen what you have said. You have just made a bad **reputation** for someone who could be a co-worker or your future boss. Matt, you have to think before you post things, or you could get into serious trouble." I'm feeling deep remorse inside me.,

"Henry, I am sorry for saying the things I posted. I was in the moment not thinking about the repercussions, I will go delete what I said, ok?"

"Matt, just because you delete something doesn't mean someone has already taken a screenshot or showed it to someone else. Seriously, you have to think next time".

I hate getting yelled at by someone who I care about.

"Ok, I understand."

"Alrighty, I will talk to you later, bye," then Henry hangs up the call.

Henry is right. I shouldn't have replied to this stranger in the first place. Being in the moment, you say things that you don't mean. You don't think about who is reading what you are posting. It could be a family member or a close friend that could have a negative image of you based on what they saw. While social media is a beautiful thing, it is also a dangerous game that you have entered. You are the player that they want. You must keep your status up by posting risky or sexy photos. If you don't hit a certain amount of likes or comments, your status will fall. You might think you are always right, but someone is waiting to write a negative comment about you. Congratulations, you are a slave to social media.

10
See You Next School Year

Today is the last day of my first year of high school. It is a half-day today, so the whole school will get out by noon. I am supposed to bring $5 to school today for the picnic lunch that they are holding. It is nothing fancy, just a hot dog, with chips, cola, and a cookie. I guess it's a step up from meatloaf day, so I applaud. I start to get ready for school and am looking at my closet. I decide to wear a sleeves Hollister tank top with tan shorts and my Nike zoom black shoes. I am heading downstairs, and I see my mom making breakfast.

"Good morning, mom, how's it going?" I ask in a pleasant tone. She looks up and says,

"There is my soon to be sophomore, sit down, eat." I see that she has laid out an egg omelet with bacon and a side of chocolate chip oatmeal with a glass of skim milk. I sit down at the end of the table, and my mom is on the other end.

"Would you like to do anything this summer?," my mom asks as she is picking up her glass of water. I take a couple of minutes to give it a thought. I reply to her with a hesitant tone,

"I would like to go to San Diego." My mom considers it then ask,

"What would you like to do in San Diego?" I tell her I wouldn't mind going to the beach, Seaport Village, and to see the U.S.S. Midway. My mom nods and seems intrigued.

"Well, I will keep that in mind," she says with a smile. I notice the time, and it is seven twenty-one. I jump up from my seat and head to grab my backpack set by the door. As

I open the door, I faintly hear my mom say, "Love you, have fun."

I see the seniors wearing Hawaii themed shirts as I arrive at school. On their last day of high school, the seniors host breakfast while wearing Hawaiian theme clothes. As I am walking up the front steps of the school, I mutter under my breath,

"lucky bastards, I can't wait to get out of this place." I walk through the double doors of the school, heading to the group's table. As I am sitting down, I say in a happy tone,

"Happy last day everyone."

"Yeah, last day until August," says Nick as he rolls his eyes.

"Yeah, but we are finally going to be sophomores, how exciting." Nick says with an irritated tone,

"great, we get closer to take the A.C.T. and stress ourselves out even more." I look at Nick and yell,

"Bruh, stop being so negative," with an irritation tone. A moment of silence goes by, then Henry asks,

"So, does anyone have any plans for the summer?" We go around the table to find out what each summer plans are. Calvin plans on traveling to Colorado for his internship. Nick is going to work at the movie theatre. Henry is going to head to Europe for a few weeks.

"Well, it looks like it is going to be a busy summer for all of us," I tell them.

As we are heading to history class, Mr. Smith is waiting outside the door with a piece of paper in his hands. As we arrive to do the door, he hands us one slip of paper and tells us not to write on it yet. We are waiting for everyone to arrive. Mr. Smith closes the door and begins to walk down the aisle wants us to tell him what we are going to do this summer. He gives us twenty minutes to write down what we are planning on doing. Once the twenty minutes end, Mr. Smith says,

"okay, we will start at the front of the room, and I would like you to stand up and project your voice to the class." Do we have to try and compete against each other to see who has the better summer? As students are sharing, you can tell from people's facial expressions your summer will be amazing, or it will suck.

After everyone shares their plans for the summer, we hear a long beep on the intercom. "Good Morning students, today is the day we have all been waiting for... last day," the principal says as he is breathing heavily into the microphone. He continues,

"Let us wish our seniors a bless life full of great things to come their way." A moment pauses, and he says his final words to the seniors,

" Seniors, for one last time, you are now dismissed" with a blissful tone. The whole school so quiet that you could hear a pin drop. Then out of nowhere, we hear screams and people going crazy. The underclassmen come out of the classrooms to watch the senior class walk down the hall for one last time. We start clapping and cheering for them, but I want to flip them off because I am jealous. We head back into the classroom, and our principle comes back onto the intercom,

"Underclassmen, have a great summer, be safe, and we will see you guys in August." The intercom is still left on, and we hear faint sounds of music playing. Schools out by Alice Cooper begins to blare throughout the school building. We run out of the building towards the picnic area. Everybody grabs lunch and sits on the wooden benches. I can't believe that we have completed our first-year high school. Once we finish eating our delicious five-course meal, we head towards the busses. Before getting on the bus, we look at each other, and Calvin yells,

"let us try to hang out this summer." We all agree, but let's be real; it won't happen. It's summer; it is our time to get away from schoolmates. As the buses start to pull away, I yell,

"see you later, sophomores." I see everyone waving goodbye to each other as we part away from each other. This is how real friendships are made. Not by the big moments, but with the little ones. Trust me, I will never forget this moment.

11
Sophomore year

My mom and I arrive back on the front steps of our home from our fantastic trip from San Diego. We went to Oceans beach, to the U.S.S. warship, traveled up to see the Hollywood sign in Los Angeles, and many more exciting things. It is a shame that school starts tomorrow or I would have stayed longer. Within a few seconds of being in the house, my mom asks me to put my suitcases in my room. I have two big orange bags. I'm almost to the top of the staircase when I miss the last step and tumble back down. My mom comes running frantically into the room.

"o my god, Matt, are you ok?"

I tell her in a defeated voice, "This is why I hate stairs; they are the devil's work."

She helps me up and takes one of my suitcases. We both head upstairs to place my bags under my bed. My mom sighs with relief and says,

"Ok, I will head to the store to grab us some food." She heads downstairs to grab her car keys then I hear the door shut. The house is quiet since Spike is at the kennel until tomorrow. With all the travel we have been doing, I am so tired. I climb into bed and begin to fall asleep.

I wake up in pitch black, trying to figure out what time it is. My phone displays 8 P.M, god I love power naps. I hear the T.V. running from downstairs, which means mom is back from the store. I see my food waiting at my placement. My mom says,

"Hey, sleepyhead, you should probably warm up your food; it has been sitting there for a while." I grab the food of the placement and head over to the microwave. As the humming of the microwave continues, I walk over to see my mom is watching Keeping Up with the Kardashians for some odd reason.

"Mom, why are you watching this? You always complain about how fake and plastic they are." She nods her head and says,

"Yeah I know, they are so amazing." I couldn't disagree, they are such an iconic family, and I wish one day I could meet them. While I am waiting for my food to cool down, I run upstairs and grab my phone. I head back downstairs to sit at my dinner placement. While I am checking my social media Instagram shows me that I have gained 13 new followers. I notice that some of the followers are from school, while others are ghost accounts. I finally have triple digits on my account. I check Snapchat to see that I have gained 5 more', friends.' I add them back within a heartbeat. At this point, I don't care who you are as long as my numbers are higher than yours, I am happy.

After I finish up my meal, I walk over to my mom to give her a hug. I tell her that I am still very exhausted and want to go to bed. She says,

"ok sweetie, sleep well, and be ready for your first day of sophomore year, how exciting." Yeah, how exciting to start another year at the same school with the same people who I still don't know. While I am getting ready for bed, a thought comes to me. We are only three months away from figuring out who the next President of The United States will be. I am not ready for these next three months of yelling back and forth and the stress that will follow. I begin to doze off. The next thing you know, I am dead asleep.

Beep *Beep* *Beep*, I try to grab my phone while my face is in the pillow. I had a hand on it, but then dropped it. Now the alarm is beeping under my bed. I turn over onto my left side and was trying to reach my phone with my right hand.

"Damn it, come on," I say with an irritated tone.

"Ah-ha got you," I bring it and place it on my bed. Since the new school year has arrived, I want to flaunt what I bought this summer. It is nothing fancy as I bought new clothes from the mall. I decide to wear a red and white sport shirt from Lacoste with black shorts and my Nike running shoes. I felt like a real athlete today.

After not speaking to my classmates for a few months, they all begin to ask the same questions.

"O my God, Matt, how's it been? Or "How was your summer?" My favorite one is, "I would love to hear about your summer." You don't love to hear me throughout the school year, so why now? While I am in the cafeteria, I see the freshman looking scared. I walk past them, muttering stupid freshmen under my breath. I notice that the group is sitting at the same table. It is a little weird seeing them because they all look a little different. Nick looks like he hit the gym pretty hard while Calvin grew out a beard, and Henry changed his style from mix to match. I walk up to the table and say with excitement," My dudes, how the hell are you?" They look up and say together,

"Matt, what is up" with such enthusiasm. I sit down, and we begin to share what we did over the summer. I share with them that I went to San Diego. Nick worked all summer at the movie theatre. Henry went to London,

Germany, and Switzerland. Lastly, Calvin shared with us that he shadows a plastic surgeon for 8 weeks. Our conversation dwindles down when we hear the dreadful sound of the bell. As everyone is getting up,

I ask the group what classes they are taking. Calvin tells me he is taking an art class. Nick is taking calculus, and Henry is taking P.E. My stomach drops a little bit as I realize that we don't have any classes together. As our eyes pounder around, I ask,

"do we all have the same lunch?" Everyone double checks their lunch schedule and says yes. Well, at least we will have lunch together. Cherish every moment you can get with friends, even if it is for a couple of minutes.

After a boring class of statistics, it is finally lunchtime. Today the cafeteria is serving mini corn dogs with green beans and fruit. I grabbed my lunch and walked over to the table. I put my trey down and say

"I have never seen it this packed before." Nobody responds to me, so I ask,

" What is with the long faces," I ask. Nick replies with a sad tone in his voice,

"I hate not having you guys in my class; it's just not the same." Calvin and Henry nod in agreement. I understand where they are coming from, but we are here now, so let's make the most of it. As we chat about who we think is hot, the bell goes off. We all get up from our seats to head back to class.

It is two-thirty, school is getting out. I exit the building to see Henry sitting on the bench. I scream his name in a high pitch voice. He looks down as if he is embarrassed to be associated with me. As I approach him, he asks with an irritated tone,

"Why do you sound like a little girl" I lean in and tell him,

"You better best bet I'm the prettiest little girl that you have ever met." We both begin to laugh, trying to figure out what has been said. As the laugh dwindles, Calvin and Nick head our way. While Calvin continues to explain to Nick the difference between there versus their, I see a perfect opportunity for a photo. I interrupt their conversation,

"You guys, let's take a photo." Henry is a party pooper and says,

"Matt, we see each other all the time we don't need a photo."" I reply with a sorrow tone,

"but the memories, do it for the gram." With some resistance, he finally agrees to it. I ask the student who is walking by to take our photo. We are sitting on the bench with our fake smiles, waiting for the countdown. 3..2..1.. say "cheese." After we hear the click of the camera, we immediately drop our smiles. I thank the student as he hands my phone back to me. The group huddles around me as we review the photo. As we are looking at the picture, I notice that Henry didn't smile.

"Henry, why didn't you smile?" I ask curiously

"I don't smile in photos, and it's pointless to put on a fake smile for three seconds then go back to your resting bitch face."

I understand where his point of view is. I can't tell you how many times I have put on a fake smile for the camera. I hide the pain that I am feeling with a smile so no one can tell that I am struggling. After we are doing reviewing the photo, I let them know to send it to them tonight.

My mom must be home early as I see Spike waiting on the lawn. I walk into the kitchen to hear my mom is talking to another co-worker on the phone. It sounds like they are shit-talking their boss hardcore. As I am heading towards the refrigerator, I hear my mom say, "Ok, shelly; I should probably go as Matt just walked in" My mom hangs up the phone and gets up from the chair.

She switches to her momma bear voice,

" Hi sweetie, how was school?"

"It wasn't bad."

I open the fridge to see that it is half empty. There is only fruit, a half-open can of Pepsi, and eggs." When are you planning on going to the store?" I ask curiously

"I will go tomorrow until then. I think we be fine."

I don't think she has seen the fridge yet, but ok.

She walks over to me while holding her phone.

"Did you see this hilarious video?" She shows me her phone.

"Yes, mom, I already saw it two days ago, get with the program."

"Well, sorry, Mr. Popular, I will try better next time," she says with sarcasm as she looks back down at her phone.

There is a brief moment of silence when my mom looks back up with a concerned face.

"Matt, tell me the truth, how are you feeling?"

"I'm doing well, just tired."

"and how about your social media, how is that?"

I hesitate because I am not sure if I should tell her about the rude comment I received by this troll or not.

"It is going well," I say with a smile

I can tell she knows about the comment, but I don't want to worry about her. I break the silence by showing her the photo I took with the group.""Mom, check this out," I said

"What is it?"

I pass the phone to her, and I can tell that she is happy with her reaction.

"Aww baby, that is so cute," she says,

"I am so glad that you found a good group of friends."

She hands me back my phone and begins to head up the stairs.

I am feeling exhausted, so I head back to the couch. I grab the small grey throw pillow and a small blanket off of the other furniture. As I am lying down, I check the photo one more time. To me, this is more than just a picture; it is a treasure. I see a new family that I don't want to lose. While it was rough at the start, I found myself growing as a person. I find myself trusting others more and being more appreciative. I feel more confident knowing that it's ok to make mistakes because I have a support team behind me ready to help out. Before I turn off my phone, I head to Instagram to post the photo. I caption the photo,

"This isn't what friendship looks like, this is what family looks like."

I tag the group into the caption, heading down below. I hit the submit button. Within two minutes of posting the photo, I see that Henry and Calvin liked the picture. I couldn't help but smile from ear to ear. As I am about to fall asleep, I put my phone underneath the pillow. As I am drifting away, I tell myself that I am a great person with great friends, and nothing will get in the way of ruining this friendship.

12
The Election

I wake up to the volume of the TV is turned on. Apparently, my mom didn't see me on the coach? If she had been sleeping on the couch, I would have watched my show somewhere else. I stretch my body on the sofa and release a couple of yawns. My mom turns her head and says,

"o sweetie, good morning, you startled me." I look at her with a dead face.

"What time is it?"

"It is six-thirty a.m"

With a confused tone, I say,

"No, are you serious?"

The T.V. is playing the morning news shows. I can't believe I slept on the couch all night. I try to grab my phone, but I can't underneath my pillow. I jump up from the couch, throwing my blanket and pillow into the air. I still can't find it, so I start removing each couch cushion one by one. My mom looks at me and says,

"Matt, what are you doing, don't ruin the couch." Sorry mom, but my phone is more important than your couch.

My phone is still not there. I ask myself, where else would my phone have gone? My eyes wander until I see a side crack on the couch. I come up to the side and put my hand down through the break.

"Ah-ha," I yell with an undefeated tone when I felt my fingertips hit the phone. After a couple of tries, I finally have my full hand on the phone. I bring it up and brush the dust off of it. My screen comes on, and I see many notifications from news outlets. I unlock my screen to read the headlines title Presidential Debate Tonight. I can't believe we are getting closer to be electing the first female President, and I am going to be around to see it happen. As the news outlets are discussing whom they think will win the debate tonight, my mom shouts out

"Trump, motherfuckers."

I look at her with my mouth open.

"Jesus, mom, what the hell was that?"

"I'm sorry sweetie, I hate how they think Hillary is the best," says my mom.

"These news channels think that Trump is the worst ever, but he is the best thing that has ever happen to this country."

I am biting my tongue to the point where I feel like it is about to fall off. Is he the man that our country needs? I don't know what to think anymore. All I can think is that tonight is going to be one hell of a night.

I can hear my mom blaring God Bless America around the house as I am getting ready for school. It is a good thing that she is singing inside because she is no Adele. I head downstairs to hug her before I leave for school. I yell, "mom," but she can't hear me. I get closer to her phone, and I turn off the music. She turns around and says,

"Matt I am listening to that, put that back on"

"I will once I get a hug, I am about to leave for school."

She hugs me and then puts the music back on. I head out the door.

I arrive at school to see people wearing red hats. I put my head down and continue to walk to the cafeteria. I understand that there is a group of people wearing red at the table. I approach the counter and politely get their attention.

"Hey guys, I'm sorry, but I have a group who usually sits here." They lift their heads, and I can't believe what I am seeing.

"I told you he wouldn't know it's us," said Nick as he laughs.

"What the hell are you wearing?"

"Don't you like it, we received them in the mail yesterday." I look at them with such disgust.

"Guys, please take them off."

Henry gives me a little attitude and says,

" Why should we, freedom of speech little snowflake,"

I am debating whether I should leave or stay. As we are looking down on our phones, I say

"So, tonight should be interesting, am I right?"

"Yeah, it is going to suck for the liberals," replies Calvin.

"What do you mean?" Calvin looks up from his phone and stares me dead in the eye.

"Matt, Hillary has no chance of beating Trump in a debate. Trump is going to walk all over her"

I nod my head as if I am listening, but I wasn't. After he is done rambling on about how great Trump is, I say with a condensing tone,

"Well, who knows, we will see tonight what will happen." All I know is that our group is about to get heated.

As time goes by, the sky turns from bright to dark. The debate is about to start in a matter of minutes. I proudly put on my I'm With Her shirt. We have the family T.V. channel on

NBC as we begin to wait for the debate to start. My mom orders pizza, so she doesn't miss anything. We have our eyes glued to the discussion. Without looking at me, my mom says

"How exciting is this, the final debate" as she is rubbing her hands back and forth.

"I guess, but if it's like the last two debates, we are screwed," I tell her as roll my eyes.

"Well, I hope that they will act like adults this time."

A moment of silence hit the room, soon followed with a burst of loud laughter.

I tell her how funny she is as I am coughing and laughing at the same time. The news stations begin the debate. We see Hillary walk out and I yell,

"There she is the first female president" with such excitement. My mom scoffs. Then we see Donald Trump, and my mom yells,

"The soon to be the best president ever."

I look at her and think you are so lucky to be my mom. I hear the group chat blowing up my phone. I see Nick wrote that Hillary is going to lose, and the other two agreed with him.. I carefully think about my words and say,

"we will see my friends." I put my phone on do not disturbs so I can pay attention to the debate. I see Clinton destroy Trump with his sexual assault accusers while Trump talks about Clinton's emails. At this point, this is not a debate. These are two children, I mean adults, picking at who did what rather than the issues that we want to hear.

When the debate ends, my mom and I conclude that it was like an episode of Keeping Up with the Kardashians. It was filled with so much hate and drama I pick up my phone to check the group chat. I begin to type,

"Who do you guys think who won?" I see that all three of them are typing. Nick writes, "Harambe." Calvin writes the "Hobo on my street," and Henry writes his "mom's leftover meatloaf." I can tell everybody was feeling the same way about our choices. It is only a couple of weeks until history is changed forever.

****

I'm awoken from my sleep when I feel this person jolting me as if I am in an earthquake.

"Matt get up, today is the day," she says with excitement.

"What is happening"?

"Today we get to elect a new president of the United States," says my mom

" Now get out of bed and get ready for school. It is going to be a long day, mister."

I can't believe that today is election day. After months and months of yelling and attacks, we are finally here. Let's just pray America votes the right person in.

I arrive at school to see segregation at its finest. On one side, I see red hats on, and on the other, I see a few students wearing blue. I feel like I am a part of the civil war. I head over to the table to feel many eyes watching me.

"Matt, everyone is looking at you," says Calvin he is embarrassed to around me.

"Should they be surprised?" I chuckle.

As I get ready to say something else I hear someone say,

"Hillary's career is over with."

I don't turn my head because I don't want to give in. I muffled under my breath,

"screw off, dumbass."

I am starting to get a little irritated by people coming up to me and saying ignorant things. I calm myself down by telling myself that this will be over by tonight, and I will be the one who is laughing in the end. I ask the group,

"Do you want to watch the election together?"

Nick immediately says,

"Hell no, I don't even want to be in the same room with your snowflakes." I stare at him and shake my head.

Calvin takes a look at me and says in a baby voice,

" Aww, the snowflake is already getting upset."

"Dude, shut up, ok." He can tell that I am serious, so he backs off.

The bell rings, and we head to our classrooms.

As we are walking, I say,

"I guess the next time I see you guys, we will have a new POTUS."

"Hell yeah, we will," said Nick with such energy.

Henry insists that our group chat will be heated tonight, but I disagree with him. I am going to try to avoid the group chat at all costs tonight.

The most important night in every four years is finally here. My mom and I are sitting on the couch, not wanting to move a muscle. We begin to see early exit polls, and it shows the Hillary is leading.

"Come on, Hill," I am yelling while clapping and standing up.

"Matt, you know those are early polls, they don't mean anything."

I stop clapping and sit back down. I hear my mom released a soft chuckle.

It is nine o'clock now, and tensions are starting to grow. The new casters keep projecting new states that both candidates have claimed. I notice that the newscasters are calling more states for Trump than Hillary, I begin to feel sick. The group chat notifications are blowing up my phone once again. I open to see what they are saying, and it is what I expected.

Henry asks if I am going to cry tonight. Then Nick tells me how I should feel ashamed of being a part of the loser party. Lastly, Calvin insults me by calling me dumb like my party. As I am reading these, I am starting to get upset. I don't type anything for a couple of minutes. Once I collect my thoughts, I begin to type, "Guys, it is still early Hillary can still win Pennsylvania, Michigan, Ohio, and Florida."

I see that Nick sees what I wrote and responds with a laughing emoji. I throw my phone on the other couch so I don't say something that I would regret.

It is now midnight, and I am losing more hope as time passes by. I see my mom smiling from ear to ear as she shouts Trump!, Trump!, Trump!. At this stage of the election night, Trump is a couple of states away from hitting the 270 marks. I have no words to describe how I am feeling. Soon we see the newscasters project the news that many Americans were not ready to hear.

Headlines across every news outlet state, "We can project that Donald J. Trump will be the next President of the United States of America." My mom screams with joy while I am sitting in a chair with chills. I'm not trying to believe the news. I don't even attempt to look at my phone because I know it wouldn't be fair. I'm hoping that this isn't true, but it is. Two thoughts came into my mind while I am contemplating what I just heard. The first thought is what the hell has happened to our morals and values. The second thought is how am I going to show up to school tomorrow; I am going to be the laughing stock. I decided that it would be best for me to leave the room. I tell my mom,

"Well mom, congratulations, I'm going to head to bed."

"O, sweetie, don't be upset, be" I stop her abruptly and wish her goodnight.

She nods her head and turns back to the T.V. While I am lying on my bed, I can't wrap my head around what has just happened. I am trying to think about what could Hillary have done to defeat Trump. I couldn't think about it anymore, or I would have gone insane. As I am about to fall asleep, I begin to feel uneasy about the thought of tomorrow. I know that I am going to get harassed and teased. I am not mentally ready for what is about to come next.

13
So It Begins

It is the morning after the election, and I don't want to get out of bed. I slept horribly last night because I am worried about what the day will bring. I start to get ready for school. Instead of wearing something fashionable, I decided to wear sweats with a plain white tee shirt with a hole near the armpit. I tell myself that I will not mention anything about the election at school. I head downstairs and see my mom making coffee. My mom looks up from reading the newspaper and says,

"There is my handsome little snowflake, how are.." then she notices what I am wearing.

"Uh, Matt, did you get attacked by a raccoon?"

I say in a condescending tone, "What do you think?" She presses her lips together and shakes her head.

"Matt, come on, it will be okay, this country will be better than ever before." I don't even say one word. I grab a granola bar out of the pantry and head to the bus stop.

As the bus is arriving at school, I sink in my seat. I don't want to be here. The bus comes to a stop, and everybody rushes to get off. I wait to be the last person to get off the bus. I can feel the eyes lay upon me as I walk into the building. I can hear the whispers hitting my ears. I feel like a thousand eyes are upon me. I keep walking with my head down. I am about to sit down until I hear someone say, "This is Trump's country now, get them out of here." I turn around and yell,

"How about you get out of here, you freak." I sit down at the table to see the group look at me with confusion. Henry begins to speak,

"I am surprised you are here matt, I thought you were going to pretend to be sick. I laugh out loud and tell him that school is important to me. The group shrugs their shoulders and continue to play on their phones. I keep asking God to help me get through this day. As we are sitting at the table, some random kid whom I have never spoken to comes up behind me and grabs my shoulder. He squats down to my level and says,

"I wouldn't want to be a part of your party today, faggot." The group puts there phones down as this is happening. I turn to see who this person is. It is Cameron, the most prominent conservative of the school. They can see I am starting to get angry by my face expressions. Nick steps in and says,

"Guys leave him alone." I mouth the word, thank you. He continues to speak,

"He has suffered a lot within the past 24 hours, he and his snowflake buddies are sad." I throw my hands up in the air. The table is filled with laughter. Is he serious right now? I shake my head with careless.

"Alright I think it is time for me to go, I will see you at lunch." As I am getting up Cameron's shoulder checks me and says

"Don't cry too hard, little bitch" As I am walking away, I give Cameron the longest death stare.

The group sits there without saying a word. As I am heading towards the bathroom, I begin to feel an overwhelming feeling of sadness. When I enter the bathroom, I go into the stall. I close the door and hit my head against it. I turn my back around while looking at the ceiling. Is this how my day is going to be? I remind myself that I will be out of here in a couple of hours. As I am clearing my thoughts, I hear the bell ring. I open the stall door and head to class.

I am the last one to arrive in the class. I can sense everyone looking at me, but I don't say a word. I sit down at my desk to see a piece of paper on it. I swipe it off my desk and begin to read it. The note read, "Liberals like you need to die." I look up to see who wrote it, but I can't tell. Everyone is either looking at the professor or on their phone. I rip up the note into small pieces and brush it onto the ground. I lay my arms across the desk and rest my head on them. For the remainder of the class, I didn't pay attention to the teacher. I just want to go home. The moment the bell rings for lunchtime, everybody gets up in a hurry while I am still lying at my desk. The teacher comes over to me and puts her hand on my shoulder,

"Matt, it is time for lunch."

I get up from the desk with my head still down and leave the room. I arrive in the lunchroom where I grab a bag of chips. I sit down at the table.

"O, there's Matt, we were wondering where you were," said Henry. I don't lift my head or say a word.

Nick, see how I am feeling.

" Aww, is Matt sad?" I finally look up and slam my hands down on the table,

"Shut the hell up, I have had enough of your bullshit from you and everyone else!" At this point I am furious,

"Yes I get it, Hillary lost, I don't care as much as you think I do now just stop being annoying." As I am yelling, I didn't realize that the cafeteria got quiet. I turn around to see people with their phones out, looking at me. Great, just what I need is for people to talk about how crazy I am even more. This is what I wanted to avoid. I grab my chips from the table and left the cafeteria. I go outside to get some fresh air. I don't want to be here anymore. Just a couple of hours, Matt, you can do this.

It the end of the school day, and I see the busses pulling into the driveway. As I am waiting for the busses, I see Henry, Calvin, and John altogether. They look over at me with disgust. I put my head back down and begin to tear up. I don't know why they are mad at me when they kept antagonizing me. I am the punching bag, but yet it's my fault? I am confused. I hop on the bus and sit where I usually sit. I see other students come on, and I see Cameron in line for this bus. My stomach dropped so quickly. He comes up the stairs, and we meet the eye to eye.

"O my God, no way, the liberal fag is on here, since when?" I try to ignore him, but he comes up to my seat.

" psst, boy, you had some real balls for standing up against your friends." He picks my head up by the hair.

"If you ever try to stand up to me, you won't stand ever again, got it little bitch."

As he lets go of my hair, he pushes my head towards the window. My head hits the window pretty hard. The bus driver yells,

"sit down; we are about to move." Cameron gets up and heads to the back of the bus. Throughout the bus ride, I am feeling sick to my stomach. I arrive at my bus stop. I get up from the seat, and as I begin to walk I hear someone yell,

"Hey, dumbass, watch out." I look behind me to see who said that, and as I do, a water bottle hits my head. I rub my head vigorously. I hear Cameron and his crew laughing. The bus driver sees it and says,

"Hey, stop it right now." I exist off the bus tearing up once again. I feel like I am walking the walk of shame to my house. I did not ask for this to happen to me. At least I will be safe at home.

I arrive at the front steps of my house after a long walk. I open the door to the smell of Italian food being cooked. I walk into the kitchen with shrugged shoulders where I see my mom making Italian meatballs.

"Matty, how was school today?" I want to tell her it was hell, but I know she would want to know why.

"Yeah, it was fine, nothing new." She smiles at my response. I sit down on the sofa and exhale a deep breath. I shouldn't have done that because she looks up with concern.

"Are you okay, Matt?"

"Mom, I already told you yes, I just.. today was a long day, okay." I know she can sense something, but she responded with a-okay. A couple of minutes past and I feel like I need a nap. As I begin to head upstairs, I say

"I am going to take a little nap."

"Okay, I'll call you when dinner is ready."

As I am in the room, I have the urge to share my pain with people. I open my social media apps. I take a photo of my face with a tear rolling down my face. I filter it with black and white. I think about a caption for this photo. I caption it as I'll be okay, and I hit the submit button. After a couple of minutes of waiting, I see my comment, "O my god. I hope you are okay." Soon I see alike and another comment, "Matt, are you okay, just know that I am here for you." I scoff at that one because people say that, but when you need them the most, where are you now? As I am reading more comments, the more I break down. Why couldn't you have been there for me earlier today? I am lying on my bed, feeling so hopeless. Is this how every day is going to be now? Am I the punching bag for the whole school? I don't want to go back to school after today.

As I am doing this, my mom yells dinner from the kitchen. While I am heading downstairs, I try to put on a happy face. I see that she is already sitting at the table. I pat her shoulder to let her know I am here.

"O, Matt, can you hand me the cheese, please?" I pass her the cheese and try to say in my happiest tone,

"This smells so good." As we are eating, I want to make small talk, but my voice won't let me. It's as if my voice doesn't wish to release the pain. My mom is staring at me for a couple of seconds then ask

"Matt, what is wrong?" I shake my head.

She puts her fork down on the table and says,

"Matthew, what is going on?" When she uses my full name, I know she is upset with me.

I continue to eat my food. She is starting to feel like I am hiding something from her. So before she asks me any more questions, I cut her off.

"Mom, can I just go to my room, please?" She hesitates,

"Are you going to tell me what's going on?"

I look down and shake my head, no. I can feel her looking at me with rage,

"Whatever, just put the plate in the refrigerator." After putting the food in the refrigerator, I head upstairs. I am lying on my bed, balling my eyes out. I am just trying to figure out what went wrong today. First, I get made fun of then I get threatened. I can't believe that this is my life. Before I go to sleep, I check my phone. I see that the group chat is dead. Is it because of me? Do they not care about me anymore? I am scared. I feel so alone and weak. I don't know whom to talk to. I end the day by putting on sad music and crying myself to sleep once again.

14
The Last Straw

I have no motivation to get out of bed this morning. I know if I don't get up, my mom will check on me. So I get up to turn on the shower, but I didn't get in. I look at my reflection in the mirror, trying to hold back the tears. I feel like I'm at the lowest point of my life right now. I turn off the shower and head to my closet. I grab a black shirt with black sweatpants. Don't care that my hair looks like it got struck by lightning. What is the point of trying if people aren't by your side to share the moment? After I put on my attire, I lay on my bed and begin to cry. I feel like my mind is shattered into a million pieces. As I am weeping, I hear my mom walking in the kitchen. I come up from the bed, wipe my tears away, and head downstairs.

"Hi, mom," I say in a shaky voice.

"Hi, sweetie I'm sorry, but I am running late for work, love you. Bye." As I see her heading out the door, I say, "but mom, I need your help." She did not hear me, and the door shut. I guess I have to go to school today; this should be fun.

While I am on the bus to school, I can't stop playing Supermarket Flowers by Ed Sheeran. I try to cry secretly, but I feel like everyone watching me. God, get me off this bus. We arrive at school, and I am the first person off the bus. I head into the building, where I see the group sitting at the table with Cameron. I guess you can replace a friend just with a snap of your fingers. I want to hide, so I went to the bathroom. As I am in the stall, I begin to burst in tears trying to sniffle quietly. I hear a group of guys come in. They are making small talk while I am covering my mouth, trying to be quiet. After they leave, I let the tears flow down. When I hear the bell ring for class, I am in front of a mirror.

My eyes are puffy, I look as white as a ghost, and my nose is super red from all the sniffling. Once I look a little more alive, I head to class. Thank god I don't have a class with them anymore. As we wait for the teacher to come, people talk amongst themselves. I grab headphones out of my bag and begin to listen to Thousand Years by Christina Perri. I lay my head on my desk again and close my eyes. What is going on? Why is this happening to me? I didn't ask for this. This pain that I have never felt before is killing me. I can't concentrate on anything anymore. I don't know whom to go to. While the asswipes and I are acquaintances, it doesn't feel right to go to them anymore. I feel so alone right now.

The teacher walks into the classroom and begins to lecture. My mentality is shallow at this point. I tell myself to suck it up, then I will go to the principal office. I picked up my head from the desk and tried to listen to the teacher. I hear her speak, but it goes out of one ear and the other. Soon enough, the bell rings over my head. This class felt like it went on forever. Instead of going to lunch, I head to the principal office. As I arrive at the office, I see Linda, the receptionist, typing away at her computer. I approach Linda's desk and begin to speak.

"Hi, Mrs. Linda," with a sad tone. She looks up from her computer with a concerned face.

"Matt, what a surprise, how can I help?" Without saying a word, I break down in tears. Linda comes out from behind the wooden desk and tries to comfort me.

"O, Matt, what's wrong?"

I try to say words, but I can't stop weeping.

"I.. I.. I want to go home," I tell her.

"Sweetie, I can't let you leave unless I get authorization from a parent." She can tell that I am in pain. We let a few minutes past. Mrs. Linda ask,

"Matt, is it ok if I call your mom?" I nod my head.

She heads over to her desk and picks up the phone.

"Hi, Mrs. Jansen, this is Linda from school I have Matt in here, and it seems like he is very upset about something." She nods her head and keeps saying I understand.

I pick up my head towards the end of the conversation.

"Great, we will see you soon," says Linda then hangs up the phone.

"Matt, your mom will be here in fifteen minutes ok, sweetie, so sit here, and I will be right back." As she leaves the room, I just lay my head on the wall and close my eyes.

The voice of some person awakens me. I open my eyes to see my mom with a worried face.

"O matt, what is going on?" I give her the silent treatment. My mom looks at Mrs. Linda and says,

"Thank you so much. I will take him home now." My mom and I walk out of the building with her arms around me.

As we are on the road, I look out the window without saying a word. My mom finally breaks the ice.

"So, are you finally going to tell me what is happening?"

"Mom, it's nothing," I say with a tone.

"No, stop saying that because it must have been bad enough for me to leave work early to pick you up." She did have a fair point. I didn't think about her schedule.

"Matt, why can't you tell me what is going on?"

I looked directly at her and raised my voice.

"Because you don't understand how hard it is to be a kid right now. We are constantly battling judgment from others in person and on social media." I continue to speak," You don't understand the pressure that we are feeling." I am done sharing who I am when I get rude comments from people who I don't even know. "You think your friends are legit until they turn into your enemy." My mom tries to interrupt me, but I talk over her.

" Someone can smile directly at you, but the moment you turn your back, they will talk shit." "People are so mean, and I just don't want to deal with it anymore, I am fed up."

My mom continues to drive, contemplating on what I just said.

"Matt, don't let them get to you, yes, kids are mean, but you are better than them" I scoff.

"See, you just don't understand" She pulls the car onto the side of the road.

"Honey, of course, I was your age too. There were mean people then and will always be." I shake my head.

"No, this is a different type of mean, the mean that you can't escape. We can escape it physically, but mentally it will always be with us." I can tell my mom doesn't truly understand what I feel until she asks me,

"Matt, why do you care about what people think about you?" Without hesitation, I let the truth come out,

"Because I don't want that feeling of loneliness to be with me every day. I want people to think of me as a cool, nice, and outgoing kid, but instead, it's negativity. I want people to see me and want to hang out, but instead, I am isolated. I want that feeling of acceptance, but all I get back is miserable and heartache." My mom looks at me as if she is ready to cry.

"Matt, you are accepted, and you don't need anyone's approval. You are perfect the way they are, and it is their fault that they can't see that bright side of you." I do not see it this way, but I continue to let her speak.

"People will take advantage of you, no matter what. That is when you need to take ownership of yourself and stand your ground. If they use you, then they aren't good people." I interrupt her,

"Mom, please can we just go home I don't want to talk about this anymore." She puts the car into drive and drives off. She keeps telling me how great of a person I am, but she has to since she is my mother.

When we arrive home, I run up the stairs without hesitation. I can't believe that this happened. I couldn't even finish a day at school. I couldn't pay attention to anything around me, but my sadness. I sit down on my computer chair and begin to think. As I am contemplating, It feels like the world is just passing by. I see cars go by, people walking their dogs, children playing in the streets. I can't stop thinking about what could I have done differently about all of this. As I continue to reflect, I hear a rapid dinging sound. My phone is blowing up with notifications. I grab my phone off the drawer to see what is happening. The notifications are coming from my social media platforms. I read the notifications, and I recognize that my name is tagged onto a post. As I wait for the application to open, I begin to wonder what could this be. The user name is C_amistheman. I did not realize that name. I scroll down to see what the post is. It is a private video of me singing in the shower when I slip and flash my butt. I sent it to the group in secret because I thought it was funny. The video has been viewed over 200 times and liked by 158. I check to see who liked the video, and I see Henry, Calvin, and Nick's names appear. I throw my phone against the wall, which makes a dent in the wall. I am trying to figure out why they would betray my trust. Why is this happening to me? Why are people so mean? I keep asking myself these questions, but no answer. After finding out about this, I message the group chat. I begin to type,

"Hey what the hell, how did Cameron get that video of me in the shower?" I wait for a couple of minutes for a response. I see that Nick and Calvin are both typing. Nick informs me that he sent the video to Cameron as a joke.

"Dude, I shared that in private, it was only for you guys" I am beyond angry. There was a moment of pause, then Nick begins to type.

"Matt, you need to understand that this is a joke. You have been such a pain in the ass since we have met you. You are constantly annoying us with questions and useless things to say. You are so uptight about everything like learn how to chill bro." I can't describe the level of anger I am at right now. I try to resist typing what is on my mind, but it is too late. My long message writes out,

"This is why I have self-esteem issues. This is why I have trust issues. You only have me around to use me. You have made me feel stupid within the group. You always have to be right, and when you are not god forbid. I thought we were actually building something, but I guess it turned into rubble. I hate myself for thinking that this could all be real. I am done with hate and lies. I am done living, not knowing who is actually going to like me for me, or just use me. I can't take this pain any longer. I have been nothing but nice to you guys. When I go off the radar for a little while, you get mad at me. I don't have to tell you every damn thing that is going on in my life. I am sorry that we met. It clearly was a mistake."

I see that Nick and Henry have read this. Before they respond, I remove myself from the group chat. Then I go to my other social media platforms and remove them as friends. I see the group photo on Instagram and click delete. You know the pain is real when you delete the memories off your profile. I notice that my follower list has gone down, which made my pain even worst. I feel like no-one wants to be a part of my life anymore. I don't know if I want to continue to be here. I am sicking and tired of living like hell day in and day out. I hate living with this pain 24/7. I wish there is a way for me to let the pain go. While I sit on the edge of my bed, a thought that begins to creep in my mind. I know that it's not the answer, but you don't have to suffer anymore. I continue to ponder on the idea while tears are falling down my face. Never in a million years would I have ever thought of committing suicide, but maybe it's the only way to let the pain go.

15
The Dream

I wake up to the sound of thunder in the distance. I try to motivate myself to get out of bed, but nothing is working. I try to tell myself today will be a good day, but I know it won't be. What is the point of getting up to be miserable? I hear the wood cracking down below me, which means my mom is up. I go downstairs with my thick fluffy blanket wrapped around me. I see my mom looking for food in the pantry.

"Mom," I say with a sad tone," I don't want to go to school today."

She closes the pantry door and looks at me.

"Matt, I am worried about you." I try not to tear up.

"Mom, I will be fine. I don't want to go to school." After a moment of silence, she agrees.

"Fine, but promise me you will be ok." I nod my head. She comes over to me to hug me. As I hug her as if it will be the last time I see her.

"I love you, just remember that," I let her go so she can head to work. The rain keeps falling at a steady rate. I see my reflection on the T.V screen. I don't know what to do anymore. I don't want to be awake right now. I wish I can fall back to sleep. I walk into my mom's room, trying to find the medicine cabinet. I open the cabinet door to find out that my mom takes prazosin. I grab the bottle and put five pills in my hand. I head back to the kitchen for a glass of water. Without any hesitation, I take the pills all at once. I feel like I am walking on thorns as I'm heading up the stairs. The thorns are cutting my life away from each step I take. I crawl into bed and close my eyes.

Soon, I wake up to odd feelings in the room I know that something is different, but what? As I am getting up out of bed, I notice something behind me. I turn around to see myself lying on the bed. I am so confused about what is happening. I check the time to see that it is the same time I am supposed to wake up this morning. I hear my mom walking around the house and soon says,
"Matt, time to get up," but no response. I listen to it again "Matt, honey, time to get ready for school." Soon I hear the steps cracking underneath the pressure. As my mom walks into the room, she says,
"Hey, sleepyhead, wake up; come on." She notices that my skin is lighter than usual. She walks over to my bed and says with a worried tone,
"Matt,"? "Matt?" She tries to shake me awake, but I am stiff as aboard.
"O my God, Matt, please wake up" with a panic voice. She drops to the floor and starts to cry uncontrollably.
"please no, god no, don't let this be real," she says as her hands are covering her face. As I am watching, I can't help but begin to burst into tears. I see her getting up from the floor to get closer to my pillow. I watch her walk over, trying to figure out what happened. She notices an edge of a piece of paper underneath my pillow. I see her hand shaking as she reaches for the note. My mom is crying like a waterfall as she opens the letter.
The letter states—

To whoever is reading this, I am so sorry. I am sorry for the pain I'm about to cause you. I didn't ask for this. I want you to know that I am finally at rest. I am in a better place. I don't have to feel any more pain. I can be who I am without the judgment of others. Where the number of likes and comments don't matter. Please do not blame yourself for this. For many days I have felt useless and degraded. I didn't want to tell you because I have seen how happy you are, and I didn't want to ruin it. Please don't be sad, be glad that I am finally free. Just remember that I will see you one day. I love you, and I'm sorry.

I see my mom hugging the paper close to her chest, balling her eyes out. I try to walk over to her, but she runs out of the room. I follow her down the stairs to see her grabbing the house phone. I can't tell what number she is dialing.

"Hello, 911, please help my son is dead, please hurry" She hangs up the phone and bows her head down. Her tears are falling on the ground like no other. I have never seen my mom so broken before. A moment passes when she picks up the phone again and dials the school.

"Hi, Mrs. Linda, This is Mrs. Jansen. I hate to be telling you this over the phone, but my son has committed suicide this morning."

While Mrs. Linda responds, my mom covers her mouth to muffle the pain that is coming out. After the phone call ends, my mom heads into her room and starts screaming her head off. Once she calms down, she comes back to the kitchen to inform family members about what has happened over the phone. I run upstairs to shake myself awake, but nothing is happening. I shut my eyes tight, hoping that this is all a dream. Instead, I open my eyes to see that I am on school grounds. I see buses pulling in and parents dropping off other students. I notice Mrs. Linda heading over to the principal. I assume she is about to tell him the news. I begin to walk closer to hear what she is telling him. The principal puts his hands over his mouth and begins to cry. I have never seen him show emotion over anything. I'm in total shock right now. The bell rings, and people head towards their classes. While I am walking in the hallway, I see the group huddle in the corner. I stop to hear what they are talking about.

"Do you think we were too hard on Matt?" says Calvin. Nick and Henry look at each other and then down at their feet.

"I really like Matt, and I hate the way we handled this situation," Henry says with a little weary in his voice.

I see Nick looking around the hall,

"speaking of Matt, have you guys seen him yet?" Nick and Calvin shake their heads from side to side. I try to let them know I am with them by yelling their names, but they couldn't hear me. I see them split up and head to class. I walk into my classroom to see that my desk is empty. The principal comes onto the intercom with a shaky voice,

"Faculty and Students, I regret to inform you of the sudden news. Everybody in the room is trying to figure out what has happened. The principal continues to speak,

"Your classmate, Matthew Jansen, has committed suicide this morning. We will try to bring you updates if we receive any on our end. If anyone needs to step out of class, please go to our counselors. I am deeply sorry for having to share this horrific news with you guys."

I see the faces of the students all in shock. Some of the students begin to cry while others leave the room. I didn't think anyone cared about me, but clearly, I am wrong. I walk into the hallway, where I see teachers and staff break down crying as well.

I run outside as quick as I can hope to leave this nightmare. I am screaming into the sky, "please let me go back home" while I laying down on the street. I close my eyes, hoping that I will be in my room. Rather than me waking up to my room, I wake up to the feel of grass brushing up against my body. I stand up to see a massive congregation under a tent. I walk over to see teachers, staff, family members, and students wearing all black. I see my mom standing by my casket while talking to a group of people. I hear people say,

"Matt was such a great guy with a great spirit" or "I wish I could've been there for him." I can tell my mom wants to find the person responsible for this and make them see the result. A man wearing a tux comes to inform the crowd that it is time for the procession of the body. The crowd parts like the red sea allowing my casket to roll it to the burial grounds. Everyone wants one last feel of me. Some people place their hands on my coffin while others kiss it. The only sound I hear is the sniffles coming from people. I have never seen this many people so sad before. Once we arrive at the burial ground, the workers ask the public to leave. Soon, the only person around is my mom while I am watching in the background. She looks down on the casket and breaks down, crying.

"Why did you have to go so soon," she asks in a weeping voice. She puts her head back up and moves back. She watches my coffin being placed into the ground. Once they are done with the burial process, my mom sits down on the park bench while holding the letter. I sit right next to her and watch her grieve. After witnessing this, I know that suicide is NOT the answer. I would rather suffer through the temporary pain versus leaving a scar amongst those whom I care about. I see my mom getting up from the bench. I follow her towards the field. As we are walking, I notice that the sensory is changing from the field of green to objects in my room. Next thing you know, I am standing in my room, all alone. My dead body is still on the bed. I come up next to the bed and begin to sob. I wish I didn't take any pills. I wish I didn't create any pain for anyone. I want to go back to my mom. While I am sobbing, I hear the voice of a man.

"Matt," he says with a caring tone. I look behind me to see that it's my dad. He is wearing a white button-down with blue jeans.

"Dad," I can't believe that I am talking to him.

"Dad, I'm so sorry for all of this." He comes up to me and hugs me.

"Matt, don't be sorry; you can still change this."

"How?"

"It is not your time yet" I look at him with a puzzled face.

"What can I do to go back?"

He tilts his head with a warm smile,

"Just go back to your bed, close your eyes, and lie down."

"Can you please come with me?"

"No, I can't, but like your note says, I will see you one day."

As I am walking towards my bed, I have a question to ask my dad. I turn around to see that he has vanished. I'm hovering over my stiff pale body. I hop on the bed, close my eyes, and lay down. I feel my heartbeat beating at a rapid pace. My eyes are moving back and forth. Soon I wake up to my body, dripping sweat. I'm breathing at a staggering rate. I check to see that it is only five pm. I get out bed to go to the restroom. I stop in my tracks to look in the mirror. I am sweaty as if I just ran a marathon. My skin looks pale white. My mouth is parched. I never ever want to do this again.

I hear a car pulling up the driveway. I check out the window to see that it is my mom. She gets out of her car and begins to head to the door. I run downstairs as quickly as I can. Without a second of her walking through the door, I stop her and give her a big hug.

 "I want you to know how much I love you." She chuckles, "Ok, what is this about?"

"Just enjoy this moment, don't worry about it," I say with a smile. We are sitting on the couch with no sounds running around the house. After a couple of minutes go by, and I tell her,

"Mom, I think I want to go see a counselor" She looks up "O, ok, I think we can make that work."

I never like the thought of telling a stranger about my life. I'm embarrassed that I can't deal with this on my own, but this can't continue.

"Can we go next week, Mom?" She nods her head.

"Yes, sweetie, I will see who I can find." I smile.

"Thank you, mom, I love you." I am so excited to change my life for the better, and I am not ashamed of seeking help.

16
The Session

It's the first morning since my suicidal dream. I wake up to the sounds of birds chirping, and the sunlight beaming through the window. I check my phone to see if anyone has messaged me, they didn't. Did I upset more people? I toss my phone to the end of my bed so I wouldn't think about it. I get out of bed to get ready for my counselor session that is later in the morning. After a couple of days of not caring about how I look, I thought it was time to change it up. I put on a beautiful black polo with white shorts and tennis shoes. I head downstairs to see my mom waiting for me.

"Morning, mom."

"Morning Sweetie, how are you feeling?" I give her an honest answer.

"I am a little nervous for this, but this needs to happen" I pause for a moment

"Mom, where did you find this 'Dr'?

"I found her on yelp." Of course, you did mom.

"Are you ready to go?" I grab a red apple out of the fruit basket.

"Let get this over with."

We are on our way to the appointment. The radio is playing some popular songs. I look out the window to see the passing of trees and parked cars.

"What a beautiful day it is, no?" says my mom. I agree it is a perfect sunny seventy-degree day.

As we get closer to the building, I can see the doctor's name on the sign.

I look over to my mom and say

"Mom, am I going have to explain to this person about my whole life?" She chuckles,

"No, sweetie, but she will want to know a little background of who you are as a person. I think that this will be good for you." I take a deep breath in,
"I guess" while looking back to the window.
We are pulling into the parking lot of the office. I start to feel butterflies in my stomach. I don't know what to expect; I have never done this before. I feel weird that I about to tell this stranger about my life. We walk into the office straight to the reception desk. My mom says,
"Matt, why don't you go sit down while I check you in." I look at the cringe-worthy photos that are on the walls. One of the pictures has a taco with a caption-Need to taco about it; you are at the right place. Another poster on the wall had an endless road with a caption. If you can dream it, you can do it. Is this place for real? Well, I am here, so it is too late to back out now.
After waiting for twenty minutes, I hear the door creaking as someone is about to come out. She is tall with brown hair with an average body. She is wearing skinny blue jeans with a black top and brown high heels.
"Hi, Matt? Are you ready?" I don't know what to say; I'm speechless for a second. What can I mean, I have a thing for tall women. My mom nudges me to get my attention.
"O, hi, yes, I am ready." I get up from my chair and head towards the door.
"I'll be waiting right here," my mom says as I walk away from her. We arrive at her too, and I can't believe what I am seeing. Bookcases are laying against the wall from one side to the other. I see a black chair in the middle of the room. Behind the black chair, I see a white couch.

"Matt, please have a seat on the couch" I sit down while she grabs a notepad and pen. She sits in the black chair right in front of me.

"My name is Dr. Heather Jolie, and for the next two hours, we will talk about who is Matt Jansen and what brings him today." I nod my head with a smile. The first question I am asked is, can you tell me about yourself? This question irritates me because I never know what to say. I begin to spit out random facts about me.

"Well, I am a student at Missouri High School. I'm the only child in my family. My mom and I have an unbreakable bond. I love popular music and nature. I like to meet and hang with people.

"Now that I know a little more about you, I would like to know what brings you in today?" I hesitate to say anything as I don't know where to begin. She says in the politest tone,

"No rush Matt, please take your time." Even though I just met this lady, I feel like I can open up and tell her everything since birth. As I am about to speak, I go back to where it all started.

"It all started once I transferred schools. I moved from a different town so at the time I didn't know anybody. I met this group of friends(or whom I thought where my friends), then we broke up because of an issue." She stops me abruptly,

"What kind of issues?" I feel myself getting a little antsy.

"Well, they started making me buy them food all the time, then it turned to movie tickets and more things. At first, it 'didn't bother me because I thought the way to gain friends you have to buy them things." Dr. Jones mouths the word no while shaking her head. She stops me before I continue to speak.

"Matt, why did you think that buying them things would make them your friends?" I take a moment to think about the question.

"To be honest, I don't know" I go on to say,

"I guess when I first bought the food, I saw how happy they were. I 'didn't want to lose happiness. I felt like I was finally a part of a group. I never really had many friends, so when they accepted me into the group, I felt like I had to earn my spot." As I begin to dwindle with what I have to say, I notice Dr.Jones is writing things down. The room is silent for a couple of seconds.

"Did you talk to them out of school?"

"I did, actually one of the friends introduced social media to me," We had a group chat and followed each other on everything."

"What happened to the group?"

"We broke up because I realize that they weren't good people, and I didn't want to be around them anymore." Dr. Jones has a surprise face,

"But, did you do anything to them?" I tilt my head slightly to the left as my eyes are looking across the room.

"I mean, I'm not perfect; I exploded my feelings and told them off. Aren't friends supposed to be there for you during the good and bad times? They should be there whenever you need the most. They are the people whom you want to make stupid decisions with because you are doing it together." I can tell Dr. Jones is happy to be getting the truth out of me. She sets her pen and pad down and leans closer to me.

"I am curious, what did you do when you left the group?" I didn't want to rethink the situation. Once I recollect my emotions, I begin to speak.

"Well, first, I deleted myself out of the group chats, o, and I unfollowed them. I don't know what it is, but when you notice someone unfollows you, it gives you a little sense of loneliness. Then, after all of that, I began to cry. I didn't know how to react. I didn't know what to do. I spent a lot of time with them, so there were many memories. I grabbed a piece of paper from the trash and began to write down how I was feeling. As I am reaching towards my pocket, I ask Dr. Jolie,

"Would you like to read it?" She nods her head and puts her pen down. I hand her the paper, and she begins to read it.

Here I am standing in front of you
Gazing into your eyes
 trying to figure out what led to this
Hoping that things will
 be the same
But I knew it wouldn't be
I need to hear I'll stay
but instead, there is nothing.
I knew that was my cue—to leave.

It's just us, you and me
As I search for my mind
I see your lips moving, but I hear the pain I caused inside, but
I want you to know

I'm sorry

sorry for saying the words that I said
sorry for not being there in your bed
sorry for hurting you instead
I didn't mean it no
I didn't mean it

I caught my self
Standing at your door
I tell myself I need you more
I knew that I couldn't be without you
I can't say that if it wasn't true
We argued on your wooden porch
I said things that I didn't mean, but it was too late.
Hate-filled the air, and now I'm scared.

We are beautiful tragedies
We knew we couldn't be
without each other
From the good to the bad of memories that we had
this one stays

You are broken
I am broken
I can only say...

I'm sorry
I am sorry for saying the things that I said
I am sorry for not being there in your bed
I am sorry for hurting you losing my head

I didn't mean it no I didn't mean it
But I know you feel ohh I know you feel it.... yeah

Oh Oh No I didn't mean it
I'm sorry
I'm sorry
O I'm sorry

As she is putting the paper down, I can see getting
emotional.
"You seriously wrote this?" I give her a little smile while
nodding.
"I was so broken at the time that I knew I had to write
something down." I can tell that Dr. Jolie is feeling sympathy
for me. I continue to speak,
 "The pain was taking over my body. It was the only think on
my mind. I couldn't focus on the real things that matter,
such as family and school work." Dr. Jolie notices that I am
beginning to tear up and grabs a couple of tissues off the
counter.
"One day, it got so bad that I didn't want to wake up ever
again. I took my mom's medicine, and I went back to my
room to fade away. Soon, I saw myself watching the pain I
caused to the people I love. I realized I didn't want to have
others suffer because I'm suffering. The pain that I am
feeling now won't last, but the pain I could've caused would
have lasted a lifetime." Dr. Jolie is trying to collect the
information that she has just heard.
"Matt, I am so sorry that you had to go through all of this. I
am glad that you acknowledge what you have said on your
part. Depending on the severity of everything that has been

said, maybe the friendship can be saved or maybe not. Just know that when you get into a situation like this that the words you say will change how they view who you are as a person. Some people are ruthless, which means they will do anything to get ahead even if that means to destroy your reputation in person or online. That is when you become stronger than them. You know what your limits are. You do not need to prove anything to anyone."

I nod my head while tears continue to fall down the side of my cheeks. We take a moment to process everything that has been said. Then Dr. Jolie asks me,

"Matt, why do you feel like you need to be liked by everyone?" I give some time to this question because even I don't know this answer.

"I think it is how I am. Growing up, I have been told that if I have nothing nice to say, then don't say it at all. So it forced me to present myself in the nicest way to people. Then that way, there is a reason for someone to dislike me. Soon I realize that this gave my' friends' a motivate to the advantage of me."

"Do you still believe that saying?" I shake my head with disapproval.

"Why?" Ask Dr. Jolie

"I have noticed that someone can post a photo online, and it could be a nice one, but people look at the smallest thing. They will start to be mean by saying, "it would be more pleasing if that person was better looking" or "this photo is crap," stuff like that. Dr. Jolie nods her head while I am speaking.

"This isn't a common person problem; I mean, look at celebrities. Ariana Grande had to disable her comments because people accused her of Mac Millers Death, or Taylor

Swift is ousted because she came out as a Democrat." It doesn't matter who you are; there will always be hateful people in this world."

While I am talking, I begin to notice where the source of my problems is coming from. Social media has connected us in many ways, but it has made us lose touch with who we are as a society. We try to show our desire for the perception of life to our' followers', but in reality, we are hiding away our pain. We have put likes before ourselves. Just think when it's your birthday, you care about the number of happy birthday comments you receive online instead of in person. We are playing a dangerous game with ourselves day in and day out.

Dr. Jolie gets up from her chair to retrieve a little red notebook that is lying on her desk. As she hands it to me, she says,

"Ok, Matt, I would like you to do something" I have a puzzled look on my face.

"Yes?"

She passes me the little notebook.

"I would like for you to write down things that you are feeling, and the next time we see each other, we can discuss it. At least I don't have to go to the trashcan to find a piece of paper. I look down at the notebook.

"Ok, this should be fun," with a smile, I say.

"Perfect, well, Matt is has been great getting to know you, but our time is up. I will call you to schedule another meeting in a couple of weeks." We both get up from our chairs and head out the door. As Dr. Jolie opens the standard room door, I see my mom reading a magazine.

"Hi mom, I'm done."

"O, wow already? That was quick" with a chuckle. My mom looks at the counselor and asks,
"How was he?" She tells her that it was great getting to know me, and we covered a lot of ground.
"Well, that sounds amazing," my mom says while giving me a hug.
"I can't wait to see him again soon, O, Matt don't forget to do your homework" says Dr. Jolie as we are exiting the building. I yell before the door shuts,
"I won't, you can trust me."
As my mom and I are heading back home, I can't stop looking at this notebook. I have no idea what I am going to put in it. I saw a cat today now I feel all cuddly inside, is that what I should write? I think only time will tell when I should write in my notebook. Once we arrive home, I notice my mom not getting out of the car.
"Uh, Mom, you going to come inside?"
"No, I have to head to work, I took the afternoon shift."
"Ok, well love you, have fun."
"Love you too, sweetie."
As I walk into the house, a feeling of tiredness comes over me. I need a nap after the day that I have had. I head upstairs to my room. I enter my room to see a note on my bed. O God, please don't be this a serious note. I open the letter, it reads-

Matt,

You are so strong for accepting your need for help. It is ok to talk about your feelings to someone. It may be weird at first, but you will find out that it helps you in the end. I am very proud of you for doing this. You will always be my wonderful baby boy.

Love, Mom.

While reading this, I am beginning to feel something. I grab my little red book out of my back pocket while I'm sitting on the edge of the bed. I write my first three words— I feel blessed- then I close the book. I put the book underneath my pillow as I slide underneath the covers. While I am lying in bed, I find myself not worrying about anything. I don't have an urge to check my phone, message people, or see what's trending. I wish this feeling could last forever.

17
Dear Future Me

I wake up to sound Spike barking in the front yard. I grab my phone off the desk to check the time.

I'm in shock to see that the time is ten a.m. I never sleep this late. I guess with everything going on, it has been taking a toll on my sleeping schedule. At least it is Sunday, so I didn't have to worry about school. I get out of bed to take a shower. Before I get into the shower, I decide to put on some music. I pick up my phone and begin to look at my artist list. After scrolling back and forth, I see the song Human by Christina Perri pop up. Have you ever needed a particular song that will make your day? This one is mine. After the shower, I put on a pair of black Nike gym shorts and an orange tank top. I head downstairs to see my mom watching the news.

"Good Morning Mom"

"Morning, Matt, how are you feeling?" I am not sure of how to answer this question.

"I'm not bad, and I'm not good, I am living" My mom gives me a blank stare before she says,

"Well, I guess that is one way to think about it." I grab a banana out of the fruit bowl sitting on the table. I sit down on the other end of the couch from where my mom is sitting. As we are watching the news, I get my phone out. Do I even want to check my social media, I ask myself? I see that my phone has a couple of notification from social media. They are new followers and a couple of likes from the previous post. I didn't feel anything when I saw these notifications. After everything I have been through, I give up on trying to impress people. I continue to scroll through my news feed. Everything is the same, same photos, same fake smiles, same comments. At this point, I am starting to wonder if I need social media. It has caused me more pain than wonders. Even though my follower list is high, I still feel very lonely. As I am thinking about this, I ask my mom,

"Hey mom, what should I do about my social media?" She looks at me with her head tilted.

"What do you mean?" I rephrase the question,

"Should I take a break from it?" She pauses for a second,

"I think that would be the best decision, but I can't make that call tor you. You have already shared your life with the public, and it's your call."

After giving it a moment of thought, I decided that it's time for me to take a break. You are constantly battling yourself every time you go on social media. I was so worried about how many likes I was receiving. I was concerned about not receiving approval from others. I was continually comparing what I have versus what someone else has. Social media changed the way I look at myself, and I couldn't let that continue. While I am looking at my home screen, contemplating about my social media applications, I begin to wonder what is going to happen if I don't post. Nothing. Nothing is going to change so drastically that we must go back to social media. Your mental health is more important than posting a silly post. Your pet photos, favorite vlogger, and followers will still be there. I hold down the application, and I see the question

'Do you want to delete this app" pop up on my screen. I click delete, and soon, the application vanishes from my phone. If I could tell more people to do this, I would. I grab the notebook and phone off the wooden table. As I am about to head out the door, I turn to my mom and say, "Mom, thank you so much mom, for being there for me. I am so lucky to have you." My mom smiles at me and says, "You are the best son that any mom could have, I love you, sweetie."

After she says that, I head out the door. Spike is sitting on the lawn. I look at my playlist to see what I'm in the mood. I click on Post- Malone, and the music begins to play.

"Come on, Spike, let's go for a run," I say with a happy tone. Once I hear the beat going, I begin to run. As I am running, I choose to take a detour from my usual route. I take a left instead of a right. I am running to the city view hill where you can see a beautiful landscape of the whole city. I see the top of the hill, and I begin to sprint harder. I knew I shouldn't have had a full sleeve of double stuff Oreos. I reach the top of the hill to feel my side hurting and hear myself panting at an extreme pace. I look up to see a breathtaking view of the city. As I am looking across the cities skylight, I notice my breathing is becoming slower. As the sun begins to set, I see the sky turning from blue to a faded pink. The city building lights start to flicker on. The tops of the buildings are flashing red. I see the street lights turn on at once. As I am watching over the beautiful city show, I realize what I need to do. I grab my little red notebook from my pocket. I sit down on the street curb with Spike by my side. I flip to an empty page. I take a deep breath within and begin to write,

Dear Future Me,

If you are opening this, that means you are in a time of need for advice. Whatever is happening in your life right now, remember that it is temporary. Nothing in life is permanent. The struggle that you are facing at this moment is not going to define who you are as a person. While life works weirdly, there is always a plan for you. If you are feeling self-conscious about how you are looking, don't. If you are worried about what others think about you, don't. Don't compare yourself to someone else. Life is too short to be worrying about how many comments, likes, or approval you receive from people. The only approval you need is from yourself. To find the light during a storm, you must clear away the negativity that is creating the storm. Don't be afraid to reach out to someone. You are strong, but even the strong need a little guidance. You are a fantastic person with such excellent capabilities. Your smile, your look, your personality are all wonderful characteristic that defines you. Don't let someone change you for the worst. Don't be fake to those who are being real to you. You will be a better person in the end. There is always going to be a battle within myself, but I will always come out on top. Now, close this book and be the person who you are supposed to be. O, before I forget, good luck on the next part of your journey. I know you will do great things out there.

After I finish writing down my thoughts, I feel my phone vibrating. I reach for It out of my pocket. I look down to see who is calling me. The number is unrecognizable to me. I click an answer and put the phone up to my ear. With a shaky voice, I ask,
"Hi, who is this?" There is a moment of silence then I hear,
"Hey Matt, it's Calvin."

Made in the USA
Monee, IL
04 November 2019

16300590R00079